THE LAST TO DROWN

LORRAINE WILSON

LUNA NOVELLA #21

Luna Press
PUBLISHING

www.lunapresspublishing.com
ISBN-13: 978-1-915556-26-4

To my fellow spoonies.

Contents

Chapter One

Tinna's aunt, near-stranger, near-silent, drove them northwest out of Reykjavik through unfamiliar tunnels that dipped beneath the sea like otters. Like hope, Tinna thought, sitting in the passenger seat. To dive into the dark with the faith that you would emerge undrowned. She watched the ocean claw at the road then retreat again, and wanted the car to stop so that she could walk down to the shore and press her hands into the water, feel the chill of it more immutable than her own self. She was not entirely sure whether she was really here or only dreaming it. Headlights flickered on with each tunnel, then off again as they climbed back up into the air, black rocks, black road, striated daylight.

'You don't mind the driving,' Lilith said eventually, when they'd left Reykjavik far behind for low coast and jagged lava fields, dotted solitary houses lying low and square against the dark earth and patches of old snow. 'That's good.'

'I don't,' Tinna agreed slowly. 'But that might just be the painkillers.'

Lilith eyed her sidelong and sniffed. 'Do you need them? You're mostly healed, looks like.'

But that had not been her first reaction, had it?

'Oh elskan mín,' she had said, materialising in front of Tinna in the airport where Tinna had faltered, clinging to her cane like a lifeline as tourists parted around her, glancing at Tinna's face and then pointedly away. Lilith had lifted one hand to touch Tinna's unscarred cheek and Tinna thought distantly that they must look bad for her aunt to show affection. Even at her wedding, Lilith had embraced her only once, briefly, like they were both made of glass.

'I'm sorry about Ben,' Lilith had said next.

And his name moved through Tinna like a storm, like a fist, like always. She shook her head wordlessly and Lilith had dropped her hand.

'They aren't for that,' Tinna said now, too slowly. She lifted her left hand halfway to her face, lowered it, thinking that surely she'd once known every single shade of black on these mountains. The air smelled like a thousand buried memories. Lilith looked at her again and she remembered to finish speaking. 'They're for the nerve damage.'

'Your leg?'

Tinna nodded.

'The cane helps, does it?'

Tinna touched her fingers to the wooden handle resting by her knee. 'On bad days.' Or busy ones, or the ones when she was too frightened of falling to trust the ground beneath her.

Lilith pursed her lips and the car filled with a sibilant wind, the studded tyres raucous then chuntering as they passed from tarmac to slush and back again. Three ravens wheeled away from the road.

'Are you supposed to be working today? I could have…'

'Caught the bus?' Lilith said disparagingly. She changed gear roughly; the car lurched, so did Tinna's heart. 'I can take the day off to collect my niece. The timing's all wrong, but there's no helping that, I suppose.'

Tinna frowned out at the grey-green land and said after a minute, or two, or three. 'You should have said not to come. If you're busy.' She wasn't even sure precisely who had first suggested taking Lilith up on the offer scrawled in her condolences card. She only remembered her mother saying she wasn't well enough, then saying she must wait two more weeks, then that Lilith wouldn't want her. But Tinna had been drifting through faded memories of black sands and the endless sea, the sharp, Arctic wind winding around her wrists, and had thought, Yes. Yes, if I must be anywhere then perhaps there, in a land made of scars and winter. And when she had returned to the present, to her mother's pale, angry face, and her brother's scowl, she hadn't understood quite what they were fighting over, and she hadn't cared. Her mother had left, and her brother had grinned at her and said, *I spent years wanting to run away back there. Shall we do it now? She can't stop us anymore and it'll be good for you.*

What about Lilith? Tinna had said, and she'd meant what if Lilith wanted her there as little as their mother did, but Elías had already been checking flights on his phone and had only shrugged. *She said you could come months ago. It was an open invitation so we can just let her know once we're booked. I'll fly with you then head back the next day.*

And because everything else felt mutable and unreal, Tinna had focused on that last thing alone. Not the going, or the questions all rusty with age, but him coming with her when he didn't need to. Survivor's guilt, she thought, was not just about surviving but about the burden of your broken self that you place upon others. If she was going to fly across the ocean into her own past, she wanted to do it weightless.

And he must have agreed because she had come alone, and met this barely-known aunt alone, and if not weightless then at least only weighing as much as her pain, and her love, not anyone else's.

'I didn't mean—' Lilith cut herself off, took one hand off the wheel and shook it lightly as if she had been gripping too hard.

A part of Tinna, a child's exhausted voice, whispered that she should not have come.

'I'm glad to see you,' Lilith said. 'I'm glad you came back. This is your home.'

But that wasn't true, was it? It had been once, and then it hadn't. They passed a weathered pillar of stacked stones like a sentinel beside the road. Tinna turned her head a little to watch it, wondering what such a guardian might be waiting for; who it was protecting, who it was protecting against.

'Your phone,' Lilith said after another tunnel, another snaggle-toothed inlet.

'My—' Tinna pulled it from her pocket, realising only belatedly that she had heard the chime. It was from Elías.

- Arrived safely? Love to Lilith. How is it being back?

Love, Tinna thought, then pushed the word away.

- Yes, she typed clumsily, left-handed. *It's cold and different and the same.* Then she ran out of words, stared at the screen for several minutes, pressed send and put it away. She was full

of things she wanted to say, if only the right person were there to listen.

They reached Snaesfellnes Peninsula just as the sun cleared a louring sky, the sea beside the road turning silver and blue, and a lone waterfall leaping from its mountain's flank like a ribbon of white hair. Tinna blinked, but time shifted beneath her like a tide and when she opened her eyes, Lilith was turning onto a track. The road slipped on away from them towards empty fields and the soft outline of scattered ruins, there and gone as the truck grumbled over the gravel and the curve of the bay hid them all from view. A black church watched them pass, Tinna's heart lurched in recognition, and then it too was gone again and the house was there instead, solid and familiar against the backdrop of the shore.

She'd lived here until she was five. Then her mother and Lilith had fought, and they had gone abruptly to London in a snowstorm and silence, but she remembered it perfectly and there was something terrible about that clarity. She'd gladly have lost this memory if it meant regaining her last months with him. But the thought was an anaesthetised open wound, both terrible and numbed, and she climbed carefully from the truck. For a moment she could hear a man weeping but it was only the wind. She turned to look across the hummocked bitter-grass to the edge of the bay, the beach of black sand and black rocks and blue-white waves breaking in permutations of eternity.

'No going in the water,' Lilith said from behind her, Tinna's bags in each hand. 'Það er bannað.' It is forbidden.

Tinna frowned faintly, looking from Lilith's face to the wide secretive sea, curling her left hand around the handle of the cane. She hadn't been thinking of swimming, but now, obstreperously, wanted to. The sea might understand, she thought—it was restless and universal and lost; it was constantly dying and being reborn.

'Come inside.'

Tinna obeyed.

'Do you remember it?' Lilith said, standing in the lounge with a cloud grey cat wending around her ankles.

'Yes,' Tinna said.

'Your mother said you had forgotten—'

'Not this,' Tinna said, feeling the wrongness of it all over again. Pain was dancing up her leg, skittering through the bones of her pelvis and spine. She'd known travelling would be hard but she hadn't realised quite how much.

'Just the few months before, is it?' The cat sat down and curled its tail around its paws, watching Tinna.

Just, Tinna thought. Just the few months before. She looked out of the window to the sea and let the words sink through her like stones.

Her phone rang as she was sitting gingerly on the sofa, and she fumbled with it in her numb right hand before managing to answer.

'You've arrived then,' her mother said. Tinna nodded very slightly, watching Lilith leave the room. 'Tinna?'

'Yes,' Tinna said, blinked and the cat blinked back, turned her head and the sea shone all silver-greys and implied darkness. 'It's just how I remember.' Which was not true, but she didn't know what else to say.

'You'll be tired. You should rest tomorrow. Stay in bed, do nothing.'

'Yes,' Tinna repeated. The idea both seductive and almost fantastical because rest was not *restful*, it was just a different balance of pains.

'Fine then. I'll speak to you tomorrow.'

The sun set slowly, later by far than back home. As if this bitter-cold, snow-draggled place was performing summertime falsely rather than barely creeping into spring. Westerly, Tinna thought. She had come westerly chasing the falling sun to the edge of a bay at the foot of a volcano, nothing but the echoes of a village and a wary black church to keep company with her family's house and the sea.

Tinna took more painkillers, then showered while the world tipped gracefully away, then wiped steam from the mirror to study her reflection. She had been told by a nurse and her mother that she would get used to this first moment of looking. But they were wrong; it had never been a shock at all. She was broken. How much stranger it would be to look in the mirror and appear whole. How much stranger if other people looked and saw someone whole. She pressed her numb right fingers to the lines of stitched skin, breathing the sulphur and salt from the shower, listening to Lilith muttering to herself or the cat.

'I'm for bed,' Lilith said when Tinna emerged. The cat was in her arms and Tinna thought that something in the way Lilith held it was more about vulnerability than affection. But the impression slipped away again like so much did, which she didn't mind at all. If she couldn't remember their last months then she didn't want to think about anything beyond them.

'Don't wander outside. Your mother says you can be absent-minded, and you have trouble sleeping.'

'Yes,' Tinna said slowly.

'Don't go out.'

'No.'

'You could have an accident.' Lilith winced, scowled. The word brushed against Tinna's damaged nerves and with this one, like with the 'just', she let the drugs carry its weight so she didn't have to.

'I've books,' she said.

Lilith stroked the cat's head then looked up at Tinna again with her face blank as the sea. 'A friend will come over tomorrow. Gerdie. She's looking forward to meeting you.' It wasn't spoken as a question but there was one there anyway, and if the drugs were not swimming through her veins perhaps Tinna would have been able to fathom it out. But they were, so she couldn't. She didn't want to be meeting strangers, but supposed it hardly mattered; her aunt was stranger enough already.

'Okay,' she said. 'Goodnight.'

Lilith nodded, threw a glance out at the sea then turned away.

And Tinna was alone, finally, in the evening half-light. The bay and the sea waited beyond one window and the dark mountains were watching her from the other. She'd been exhausted earlier but now felt beyond that, filled with a haunted restlessness that she knew too well. She tried though. Sitting and wrapping a blanket around herself that rubbed her skin like a cat's tongue, she even turned the pages of a book seeking distraction. But she'd spent too many nights walking the long corridors of the hospital, and then the dark rooms of her house to fool herself. The sun had slipped behind the great bulk of Snaesfell, and the sky was a deeper indigo than the sea as if the water still held daylight, and all of it, the mountains, the sky, the sea were safer than her own mind.

A walk, she thought, and set her book aside, ran her right hand over the cover like the words might rouse her dead nerves. A walk in the cloudy darkness. She wanted the cold to numb her entirely so that the parts of her which she could feel were rendered the same as the parts she could not. She took her inadequate, southerner's coat from its hook, left the cane behind and slipped out of the door where the mountains whispered a greeting, the sea replied, the sky above dense and imperturbable. Beneath her feet the stones were sharp and cold as ice and she studied her bare toes, surprised momentarily. Then weighing how much she cared, discovering that she didn't.

Where the shadowy grass ended, the sea was a net of black and deeper black, its whispering surf the only sound. She turned towards it but then the breeze lifted and she stumbled, knocked askew by the sudden smell of ozone and a memory. His hand on her waist, their bare skins beautified by sunshine and salt, white sand through the water opalescent, his voice still making her heart skip even then, years after they'd met. There had been children laughing away to their right, the breeze off the land scented with sage and dust, the sea like an embrace. He'd looked down at her, his eyes tawny in the sunlight, and she laid her pale hand in his darker one. *Come on*, he said. *What are you waiting for?* He'd pulled her deeper and they'd swum out past the gentle breakers. *You*, she'd said. *I was waiting for you, Ben.* The sunlight on the sea so searing she'd closed her eyes and swum to him blind.

She opened her eyes.

The sea murmured and the cold pressed against her like she was already under this black water so far from that sea, so far from then. 'I want the rest,' she whispered to the horizon. 'I want the last times, I want the worst of it all, I want every second that we had.' The night waited. 'Give him back to me,' she whispered.

It is a form of self-protection, the psychologist had said. *We seek to hide from trauma sometimes.* Tinna had said, *But I want to remember*, and the psychologist had smiled. *What we want and what we need are not always the same. Give yourself time to heal first.* Tinna might have got angry if not for the painkillers muting all her edges. Perhaps that was why the psychologist had said it.

A low voice called from the darkness, hoarse with mourning. and Tinna's whole body flexed. She almost cried out a response before she realised. 'Seal,' she said aloud. 'It's just a seal.' She'd not heard one since her childhood. and it wasn't her childhood she wanted to be remembering, so she turned sharply away from the sea and walked instead back the way they had arrived. If she kept walking, she thought, perhaps her mind would not play games with memory, it would simply drift and in drifting find lost pieces of itself. She found a track between rocks and hagged fields, half-wishing for her stick and for shoes but not enough to turn around. Then she reached a low stone wall, climbed over that onto harsh grasses and soft moss and was glad she was barefoot. Better this by far than compression tights and hospital floors.

And then the moon slipped its noose of clouds and the sky shimmered darkly, and she realised where her numb feet had brought her.

The black church waited just ahead, its steeple a sharp, starless portion of sky, its graves hunkered in the shadows, half buried. From here and in the dark, she couldn't see the lych gate or the road so it felt as if she'd arrived in some severed space, interstitial and secret. Standing amidst the graves that had gathered around her, it felt like yet another conjuring of her addled mind. She shook her head and pressed a hand against her scars, her skull, and turned back to the soft lights that she had left on in the house.

Behind her, someone sighed.

She turned quickly, too quickly, painkillers and her numb feet unbalancing her, grasping at a gravestone to keep from falling while she searched for the other person out here in the dark amongst the dead.

But the graveyard was empty. The church watched her, moonlight in its white-lined windows like a cat's wide eyes. She tightened her hold on the grave, her left hand, the one that could feel, scraping against a ragged line of white lichen like a scar; her own pulse in her fingertips as if the grave held a heart. Then the moon slunk back behind clouds and the church's eyes closed, the sky and the mountains becoming one single vast mass. Tinna wavered, her mind repeating that exhaled breath over and over, like it mattered. Like it mattered not because she was alone in this fey place, but because she had heard it before. A long breath full of endings.

Oh god, she thought, and let go of the gravestone and turned away. The night swooped around her and it took an age to find a path through the graves to the wall, headstones rearing up before her like a maze. Each one looked the same as the one that had stopped her falling. Ancient, lichen scarred, canted seaward. A few steps, ancient, lichen scarred, canted seaward. She closed her eyes and opened them again; it occurred to her that in the rush and strain of travel she might have taken an extra dose of her medicines.

But finally the graveyard released her and the moon watched her return up the track unsteadily. Then she slept in her aunt's spare bed, finally, awash with pain and hearing that long sigh in her ear. It was probably the sea ceaselessly murmuring beyond her window, but in her dreams it wasn't.

Chapter Two

'You went out,' Lilith said in the morning.

Tinna eyed the mud stains clinging to her feet and nodded. She'd been up early, taking her first dose before the pain swept her away, then standing at the window in the lounge watching the sea. A lone fishing boat had crept across it an hour after dawn, waves breaking at its prow, and those, the waves and the boat's rise and fall, made her realise that the sea was lying. It was not as calm as it seemed, hiding swell and current under a thin skin like a glamour. Perhaps that was what she was doing, Tinna thought, hiding unhealable wounds beneath a veneer of recovery, and if so who was she fooling?

'Where did you go?'

Her aunt's voice held a sharpness that made Tinna turn. 'To the church,' she said slowly, and watched Lilith's hands unwrap themselves from her waist. 'I can't sleep. Walking helps,' Tinna added.

Lilith's gaze skittered over Tinna's scars, then she closed her eyes for the length of a breath and nodded. 'So then. Not to the sea. But it is not safe, Tinna. I was serious. You cannot go out at night.'

Tinna leaned back against the window, pain crackling

down her leg. 'Walking helps,' she repeated, unable to find the words for a better explanation, baffled by something in her aunt's face that reminded her abruptly of her mother.

'So walk around the house,' Lilith snapped. Tinna blinked and Lilith said more gently, 'It's not safe. Even for someone able bodied, even for someone outside this family, there's still hypothermia and getting lost and falling in the sea. This is Iceland in winter, not Edinburgh in spring.'

Even for someone able bodied, Tinna thought, and yes, her body was unable now. It was unable to heal, or to remember, or to contain its own grief. And she was so busy thinking these things that she didn't think about the next thing her aunt had said. The stranger thing.

'I'll make us some coffee.'

Tinna turned her brittle body to face the sea.

Lilith had just handed Tinna a mug when someone opened the door, shouting a good morning into the hall. Tinna wrapped both hands around the coffee, unbalanced by the one filling with heat and the other full of nothing at all.

You must be wary of injuring yourself and not feeling it, the doctor had said. *Cold and heat particularly. Your withdrawal reflex won't work so you need to be watchful, and treat things even if they don't hurt.*

Treat things even if they don't hurt. Lilith turned towards the door and a woman swept in, all red wool and black jeans.

'Takk fyrir síðast,' the stranger said.

'Thank you for last time too,' Lilith replied, in English. Tinna unfurled her right hand from the mug and laid it against her neck, feeling the heat in it like a secondhand secret.

'You don't speak the Icelandic anymore?' the stranger said, turning.

Tinna shrugged. 'A little. I'm not fluent.' She could have said the words in Icelandic, but the woman's sharp blue gaze made her oddly nervous.

'Ach well. I am Gerdie and you are Tinna, I assume. Nice to meet you. Hvað er að frétta?'

What's the news? Tinna looked from her to Lilith, who had wrapped her arms back around herself like there was something in this room to guard against. It was only an expression. It was only an expression but Tinna wanted to laugh at the absurdity of it. She wanted to cry, but suspected she'd lost the ability.

'Coffee,' Lilith said. 'Tinna, Gerdie brought some books you might like. I—' She waved a hand loosely. '—only have boring books, she tells me.'

Gerdie sat and looked up at Tinna as Lilith left the room. 'I apologise,' she said calmly. 'I am better with my hands than with words, so if I say anything stupid then just tell me. I have a tough old hide, I can take it.' She didn't wait for Tinna to respond, but bent over a bag and pulled out, as promised, a stack of books. 'Here. Folktales, straight romance, spy thriller, queer romance, Viking saga, South Asian inspired sci-fi...' She turned over another book. 'I've no idea about this one. Consider it a mystery prize. Better than Lili's endless biographies and textbooks.'

Tinna had never thought of her aunt as a Lili; she wanted to ask who the woman was that Gerdie knew so well, but couldn't find the words. 'Thank you,' she said. 'That's very kind of you.'

Gerdie made a soft sound of dismissal. 'Lili was worried you'd not have enough to do.'

'Do?' Tinna looked away from the other woman, out to the sea. The horizon was a silver band between ocean and sky, and there were reminders everywhere but still no way of bracing yourself for them. 'I'm not sure I planned to do anything, really, just…' Rest and heal, everyone had said. Remember, she'd thought. Her gaze slipped from the sea to a flash of orange at the side of the garden. 'Maybe I could go out in that,' she said. 'The kayak. The physio said to build up exercise.' She'd done it a few times before on lakes, once a wide and friendly river.

The room behind her was silent; in the kitchen the kettle boiled and shut off. Tinna turned around.

'It's not light exercise, kayaking out there. Any time of year really, but we're barely out of winter.'

Tinna studied her right hand and flexed her fingers. 'Still,' she said. 'I might try it.' Last night the sea had offered memory.

'Try what?' Lilith came in with two mugs, set them down on the coffee table beside Tinna's. Which Tinna could not remember putting down, but there it was, slowly cooling. Her aunt shifted the pile of books and sat next to Gerdie. The cat appeared from nowhere, leapt onto the arm of the sofa and sat with his tail hanging down, studying the room unblinking.

'Kayaking,' Tinna said. She couldn't really imagine the strain and heat and energy of actually doing it, but there was something alluring to the idea all the same. To being suspended over the black deep, held between sea and sky like weightlessness. The sea might understand, she thought just as she had done yesterday.

'No!'

Tinna blinked.

'Lili—'

'Það er bannað.'

'You said that about going out at night,' Tinna said slowly.

'Going near the sea,' Lilith said firmly. 'You can't go near the sea, not until next week.' Her eyes were narrow and dark, not entirely meeting Tinna's.

'I don't understand.' Was it some law she'd not heard of? Like the snow tyres date, or the disaster alerts; was there a date too when you were permitted the sea?

Lilith shook her head, her neat hair slipping over her shoulder, silver threads catching the light. She was greying in exactly the same way as her sister. Tinna wondered if they knew that, if their mother had done the same, if she herself would. The idea of being any older than she was now was terrible.

Both women stared at her, and Tinna realised she'd spoken aloud although she had no idea how much. She shifted, pain ratcheting all along her spine, down her right leg. 'Sorry,' she said, embarrassed. 'I… what was your mother's name? I've…' Had she forgotten it, or had she never known? But that was the wrong thing to say too. Lilith looked like she had slapped her and Tinna was too tired to navigate these waters. She didn't understand why this was all so fraught, she only knew that she was making it worse.

'Come drink your coffee before it gets cold,' Gerdie said.

Tinna obeyed because she didn't know what else to do and anyway the pain meant she needed to move. She sat facing the sofa, reached with her right hand then switched to her left to draw her mug closer.

'So why can't Tinna go kayaking,' Gerdie carried on, turning her attention to Lilith. 'Aside from the obvious.'

The obvious, Tinna thought. Her scars felt like they had a greater presence in the world than she did.

'I could go out with her. It's a two—'

'No!'

Gerdie frowned. Tinna sipped at her coffee, studied the slow swirl of it as pain flickered through her pelvis and up her spine.

'Oh Lili.'

Her aunt sighed, and Tinna looked up. Gerdie had taken her aunt's hand onto her own knee, was running a thumb over Lilith's knuckles and one tiny unknown became known. The two women looked at one another, speaking a language Tinna had no part in, and then Gerdie sighed shortly and nodded, Lilith rose and left the room. Tinna met Gerdie's eyes.

'Maybe start by coming swimming with Lili and I,' Gerdie said. 'We go often and the hot pools will do you good, I'd imagine.'

But Tinna didn't want the comfort of warmth, she wanted cold to numb the pain or perhaps to crack her open and find what she had lost. Like frost shattered rocks, like glaciers calving. She drank her tepid coffee, felt herself nod as if from miles away.

Gerdie reached to stroke the cat. He arched his neck into her touch without looking, marking her familiarity more strongly than anything else. Tinna wondered why they didn't live together. Or perhaps they did normally; it was none of her business but she felt sad anyway at the thought.

'Your aunt doesn't want you to push yourself. You're barely out of hospital and we're a long way from help here. You need to keep that in mind.'

Tinna laughed, or she thought she did. The room was coruscating at the edges like the night sky and her own thoughts were swimming through the stars. She set her coffee mug down, picked up the book at the top of the pile and turned it over to read the back cover. When she looked up, Gerdie had gone and the room smelled of soup and warm bread, a radio on in the kitchen and the sound of movement beneath it. The book lay in her lap and she frowned at it, trying to work out whether she'd fallen asleep without noticing. Her leg throbbed, and when she moved the pain sharpened to a dozen blades. Drugs, she thought. She must be due the next dose, and ought to navigate her way to her feet to find her bag. Instead, breathing through the tidal yaw of the spasm, waiting for it to ease, she stared fixedly at the book.

Icelandic folktales and ghost stories. There were silhouetted animals on the cover, a mermaid that she suspected was as far from the marmennlar or the nøkker of her childhood stories as it was possible to get; silver runes around the edge, and she wondered if they said anything, or if they were like the kanji tattoos that gullible Westerners got. The back cover was full of words she had thought forgotten until she read them. The Jólakötturinn, the Huldufólk, the Selshamurinn… She thought of the sea whispering in the dark the night before, and of the way he had laughed so hard tears had come to his eyes when that fake Icelandic lullaby had spread across the internet. Sleep you black-eyed pig, fall into a deep pit of ghosts. *I'm not letting you ever put our children to bed*, he'd said.

Out of curiosity and an awareness of her own displacement, she had searched and found a real one. She'd read it out to him; he'd told her it was barely an improvement and his decision stood. '*Það er margt sem myrkrið veit*,' she whispered. There is much that darkness knows. She couldn't remember the rest, aside from the word *dauðadjúpar*. Deadly-deep. The deadly depths. She lay her right hand over the book like that might silence the world.

'Lunch,' Lilith said. Tinna's fingers tightened on the book, then relaxed again. She rose unsteadily, her body howling, and left the room in search of tablets.

She went out much later, into the slow evening with Lilith eyeing the barely darkening sky, setting her laptop aside as if she meant to rise.

'I won't be long,' Tinna said quickly, a swift flicker of annoyance in her mind but not her voice. Lilith pursed her mouth, then nodded shortly once and turned back to her work. But her fingers did not move, and the house stayed entirely silent as Tinna pulled boots and coat on and left. She didn't understand her aunt's mood and didn't want to try—a lifetime of navigating her mother had left her far too comfortable with exclosure.

Her phone vibrated against her hip when she was three paces from the house and she stood still to pull it out, shifting her weight off her right leg as she read Elías' message and replied.

- *How are you doing? Getting on okay with L?*

- *She's very like mum. I'm just out for a walk.* She went to press send, then added, *How's you?* The phone slipped within her uncertain grip and she didn't know whether she'd just rather he rang. The exhaustion of conversation versus the frustration of this thing that had once been effortless.

- *Send me photos of the beach. I want to see if it looks anything like my memories.* They had talked about Iceland to each other all the time in the year after they left. Do you remember that mud pool like a face? Do you remember my friend Gunnar? Do you remember seeing the winter fox in the garden? Do you remember bingókúlur?

Then one night they had stopped. But Tinna didn't want to think about that right now, or about anything other than this one normal thing that she could do.

- Hold on. I'll get to the shore.
- be careful
She didn't answer.
- don't fall in a troll hole.
She smiled.

*

Crossing the field to the tip of the bay, Tinna could see Arnastapi's lights across the water, coming slowly awake against the still-luminous sky, and beyond half-occluded by the coast the black silhouettes of Lóndragar rocks. She stood at the top of the grass bank and took photos that failed to capture the hollow light or the vastness. The empty sea, the bay hemmed by green lava field and the barely-there earth lines of houses long gone; the mountains louring in the dying light. She took photos of it all. They'd run along this beach, her and Elías, hunting for shells or sifting black pebbles between their hands, looking for nuances of grey and green and purple. Catching crabs in the tidepools and carrying nameless bones back up to the house like treasures to be forgotten outside the back door.

- wow. Stunning.

- yeah. It's beautiful. Which wasn't quite the right word, she thought. It wasn't powerful enough, it wasn't ferocious enough.

- do you remember?

Tinna read those three words and wanted to hurl her phone into the mercurial sea. Instead she put it carefully away, weighed the tempered levels of her pain and then walked slowly up the shore into the empty bay. Her eyes on the ground beneath her feet, or on the rearing rocks of the mountains, hemmed about with clouds of fulmar catching the late sunlight on their stiff wings. There were hollows in the cliffs like snake's eyes and the book back in the house would say that was where the hidden folk lived, the huldufólk or perhaps trolls instead, lumbering and carnivorous.

But there were only the swirling fulmar above and on the water, the black silhouettes of ducks, there and gone again between the smooth swelling waves. She thought again that it would be nice to be out there, and surely better kayaking than trying to swim. It was odd to want something, to look at the sea and think, yes, please have me. She couldn't remember the last time she'd wanted anything other than to remember.

Tomorrow, perhaps. She flexed her numb hand again, had to look at it to be sure she was doing so. When the sun slipped behind the mountains, she turned around and realised only then how far she'd come. So focused on the slip of the shingle beneath her uncertain feet, so aware of the pull of the sea that she'd not noticed the passing time. Walking back, and it was always worse walking back no matter the distance, the pain began to slingshot through her, gaining momentum with each step. She pressed her hand against her face, icy fingers numb against the oversensitive scars and walked slower, stepping more gingerly as the shadows gathered mass. The sand whispered, the waves answered, a call and response like folk song or lullaby. The sky above sank through shades of blue and the sea's voice changed, drifting through the chorus of her pain like a line of harmony. Like a voice.

Vini mínum vagga ég í ró
En úti biður andlit á glugga

The words formed in her head more clearly than any had done for weeks. Slow and deep and tidal.

Vini mínum vagga ég í ró
En úti biður andlit á glugga

Tinna stopped and turned to face the sea; the words hung like threads as if they had been sung aloud, not simply summoned from memory. She searched for understanding and found it far easier than she'd have expected.

My love let me lull you to sleep
Outside waits a face at the window.

Her mother must have sung it to her, and yet from the day they left she had barely spoken her own tongue. It was her language of extremes, of joy and anger; drunkenness, illness. Tinna's brother had spoken it more, and then they had both spoken it to her in the hospital when she was not entirely awake. Or she thought they had, she thought it had been them. Perhaps that was why it had felt so natural to come back here afterwards.

A wave caught at her feet, leaving a line of lace against the sand and soaking through her inadequate boots, the cold burning against her skin. She had not found this lullaby in that internet search, and she definitely did not remember ever hearing its tune. And yet here it was, echoing through her mind to the exact rhythm of the waves. She waited for the next wave half-curiously, aware of how dark it was becoming but not minding at all. Perhaps she was the face at the window, she thought. The lost thing trying to remember what it had been like to be alive. The water washed forward, encircling her ankles like a hand as someone sang the words again clear and slow. Tinna lifted her fingers to press against her scars, listening to a buried memory unearthed by a childhood beach and loneliness.

The very last memory she had was from three months before the crash. Them both in their tiny garden, him handing her a mug of tea. Her smiling, her turning back away. Their last text messages were two hours before the crash, five twenty-six on a Tuesday evening.

Him. *I'm outside, are you coming?*
And her. *I'm coming.*

If only, she thought for the hundredth time, she could find the key to unlocking herself. Change *something* so that she remembered those three whole months of him forgotten.

The tide whispered in the shingle and she stirred, flinching from the bolt of pain, then stilling to let it fade at least a little. She was alone within and without. No-one was singing lullabies to her in the dark. No-one was offering her remembrance or explanation, and no-one would. A wave rose and gripped her calves, her balance teetered so that she had to fling her arms out before she fell. The sea sighed, subsided.

Chapter Three

'You were on the beach,' Lilith said as Tinna entered. She was standing in the hall, a jumper hanging from her arms as if she had been halfway through putting it on. Her eyes were wide and sharp. Tinna looked at the dusting of black sand on her wet socks.

She nodded. The entire right side of her body was ablaze with pain.

'You went to the water.'

Tinna lifted her head, trying to make sense of her aunt's face through the flames licking at her bones. If only, she thought, she were in the cold sea, dark and murmurous. Tomorrow. Tomorrow she would go out there. 'Elías wanted photos.'

'You mustn't. I was serious.'

'Fyrirgefðu,' Tinna apologised distantly. Her fingers were tracing the lines where she had broken; she could feel the pathway of every single nerve.

'Christ. I should have put you straight back on the plane.'

Tinna saw from the corner of her eye Lilith's hands clenching and unclenching at her sides. She did not remember this… fear in her aunt. Her mother had said once, two glasses of wine towards honesty, that they'd fought about Lilith's refusal to sell the house. It was their grandparent's house, inherited together. Tinna frowned; the scars pulled, the nerves howled.

'Come sit down,' Lilith reached out as if to touch her, but drew back and Tinna didn't want to know why. They sat on facing chairs as they had done earlier, Gerdie's pile of books between them, the curtains closed against the gathering dark.

'Look,' Lilith said. Tinna watched her hands. They were easier to understand than faces when the pain was at its fiercest. 'I have to tell—Wait. Are you okay?'

'I need my tablets.' But she also wanted to lie down in the sea, become numbed, become lulled. Crete was about as brave as she had ever been with sea swimming, because she'd had him to swim to. And because she hadn't known then that there were worse things than drowning.

Lilith set her elbows on her knees. 'I can get them for you. Just… I have to tell you first. Tinna, there is danger in the sea here at night. You can't go out.'

'Why?' Tinna said to Lilith's hands.

Silence. Tinna closed her eyes and breathed as her nerves blazed. And in the darkness she barely caught her aunt's words.

'Her name was Astrid.'

On the table, Tinna's phone began to buzz. It would be her mother again. The calls, once weeks apart, were now almost daily, another marker of how much the world had changed. The sound threatened to judder her patched skull apart again. 'Who?' she said, her left hand bracing her head carefully.

'Your grandmother. You asked earlier.' A shadow stirred in the corner of the room, then became the cat, green eyes blinking balefully.

Had she asked? She remembered the argument about

kayaking, but not asking about her grandmother. She was too tired for this. 'Oh,' she whispered. 'That's… good to know. Look, Lilith, I need—'

'You're not… what's wrong, you look… Oh Christ, I'm sorry, I shouldn't be talking.' Lilith stood and Tinna recognised this, the near-panic of someone in the vicinity of brokenness. Not knowing what to do; wanting to help and wanting to flee in equal measure. It was the only thing she missed from the hospital, the absence of that in the nurses and doctors and porters. *Oh hen*, a cleaner had said to her one morning, *your poor face. Aye and you've had a time of it, have you not?* And even that had been alright. Sympathy without evasion or embarrassment.

Tinna got to her feet carefully. 'I need to go to bed,' she said. 'Goodnight.'

Lilith rose too, reaching out to help, or hinder. 'Don't go out again tonight. Tinna—'

As if she could. 'I won't,' she heard herself say, concentrating on the price of each step and nothing else. The bedroom swam with shadows and Tinna lowered herself onto the bed as carefully as if she were made of glass.

When she sank into sleep and painkiller dreams, the sea whispered lullabies through them all. A face waited at the window and she woke staring at its hollow eyes, the shadows beneath its cheekbones. She tried to move, to rise and close the curtain, to call for Lilith, but the drugs pulled her down again and the sea rose over her gently as a shroud.

By the time she rose the next morning, the house was empty. She studied the empty window warily, remembering her

dreams but then pushed it all aside and left the room. A note
on the kitchen counter said that Lilith had gone to work and
would be back at seven. Gerdie would come over to cook
lunch. Nothing else, nothing about the sea or the kayak, and
Tinna stood at the lounge window, measuring her pain and her
breathing. There were five stems of blue flowers wilting on the
windowsill, and Tinna studied them for a moment, thinking
that they looked familiar, that she had once known their name.
The air smelled very faintly sulphuric from Lilith's shower and
there was a dusting of snow on the grass, the mountain tops
submerged in cloud. But there was no wind and the sea in the
bay was as silver and smooth as an old mirror.

It felt like an answer to a question.

She put the sad flowers in a glass of water and ate slowly.
Elías messaged her but her mind was drifting and she could
not fathom a reply, so instead showered and dressed, watching
her numb fingers in the mirror. She could still manage nothing
more complicated with her hair than a ponytail, yet strangely,
hauling the kayak down to the shore was almost easy. It
slipped over the frosted grass like an otter, eager for the water.
And then there was just her and it, and the watchful sea, tiny
wavelets breaking at her feet like beckoning hands. This was
quite possibly very foolish, she knew that. She couldn't feel
one arm, and one leg was a morass of spasms and pain, and if
she fell in there was no guarantee she'd be able to swim even
without the rime of ice along the high tide line promising
danger.

Just for a few minutes, she thought. And now was the
best time, with her morning dose beginning to wear off so
that although the pain was mounting, so was her dazedness
retreating. She didn't trust her own body any more than she

trusted the water, but wasn't that the point? That the sea would understand what it was to return constantly to your past, sifting through the rubble of your own making searching for something new. The sea knew what it was to be adrift.

There was a fishing boat out in the open water beyond the headland, its hull painted black as a witching hour. The figure of a man stood on the open deck, watching her. Just curious, she thought; he likely knew Lilith and knew she herself was not Lilith. Perhaps he'd even heard the news of who she actually was. There'd been newspaper articles about them, back home. Brief words laden with that kind of grim dryness reserved for stories like theirs. She hadn't meant to read them at all, only a nurse had left a newspaper on her bed one day when she'd perhaps spent too long staring at the ceiling with blank incomprehension. It had likely been meant to distract her, and the nurse likely hadn't even realised the article was there, buried in the twenty-third page. They'd used a photograph from the summer before last, them both on the beach at Musselburgh, wind pulling her hair across her face and his smile like a gift. She'd felt, seeing that, a fury at the entire world for having any share of him at all.

The fisherman was still watching her, unmoving on his restless boat. But Tinna bent to push the kayak into the shallows and when she looked up a few minutes later the sea was empty once more.

It took a while to learn the swing of the paddle with one arm numb, to recognise the twist and resistance of the water in her shoulder, and gentle her left arm to compensate. The kayak yawed, making heavy work of the low swell, but she was following the shore, the water shallow enough for her to stand if the capricious beast tipped her out, and she didn't mind so much being unsteady. She had grown used to not trusting the ground beneath her, what difference the water? And then, when she was more sure of her rhythm, she pushed out a little into the blue-black bay with the strange lucent green of the lava field on one side and the black church on the other. And then after a couple of minutes she stopped, resting the paddle across the kayak and uncurling her fingers, testing them. How convoluted this thing called healing was, she thought, not for the first time. How double-sided, to feel a small spark of wary pride in herself for doing this thing; to fear that each step forward was a step away.

'I want,' she said very quietly, her voice slipping over the waves, 'what I am owed.'

She wasn't asking for miracles or for the impossible. But she was owed, surely, her own lost memories. Given everything, the very least the world owed her was the return of what was rightfully hers.

'I want,' she repeated, 'only what I am owed.'

The sea murmured, three ravens rose from the lava field calling back and forth, two of them tumbling together in a dance full of talons and love. The kayak dipped and swayed, drifting slowly further from the church's shore, towards the centre of the bay, the open sea waiting, hungry. Tinna wrapped her hands back around the paddle, the plastic a bare fraction warmer than the water running along it, but she didn't start paddling quite yet. The mountains and the bay were watchful, the grassy outlines of the lost village like the whorls of some giant's fingerprint on the land, and she tried to imagine this place when the lava had been flowing. Not black and green and ragged, but slow and ferocious, beautiful, destructive, deadly. She could imagine the lure of it, the compulsion to take just a step closer, see the heart of the world laid bare; another step, hear the hiss and rumble of it, this great serpent swallowing its own tail; another step, the heat on your skin like a promise of redemption.

The ravens called again, and she opened eyes she hadn't even realised she'd closed. The church was further away, the lava field across the water close enough now for her to see fragments of sky between the sharp skeletal rocks, and more words from that Googled lullaby came back to her.

There is much that darkness knows,
My thoughts are heavy,
I have watched the black sands burning green meadows,
The deadly-deep ice cries on the glacier.

She heard his laughter, and the ravens' laughter, and the sea curled around the kayak like a smile, a knife. This place, her childhood home, built on fury and loss, bounded by a wild and ancient sea; only today the sea was kind. It was holding her up underneath the sky like she was still something precious, despite everything. She pressed her cold left hand to her face, traced scars that were warm beneath her touch, and understood why her gaze was drawn back again and again to the lava field. How trite, she thought. How meaningless, and she shifted on the seat, releasing a wave of pain that made her hiss. She looked over her shoulder, back towards her aunt's house, and felt for the first time her own vulnerability. So far and so much effort between her and painkillers and rest. The pain danced through her nerves, her leg spasmed and she rubbed it, numb fist kneading scarred muscles, the kayak swaying half in lullaby, half in threat. The water in her shadow was as black as ink, but when she lifted the paddle, the droplets caught the light like a dozen falling moons. Come on then, she thought to the pain and empty parts of herself, it's not so far to shore. It was a lie, but sometimes that was the only way to make yourself move at all.

She left the kayak on the beach, too weak and hurting to haul it back over the grass. It canted onto its side up above the stormline where rusty kelp curled wearily, and really, who would be passing, here on the edge of an empty bay?

'Þú komst aftu.'

Tinna jerked, pain blazing up her hip as she spun around, throwing her hands out for balance. The waves hissed in the shingle. A man stood halfway between the high tide line and the water, and she squinted at him, her heart still racing too fast, the pain breaking the world into fractals so that she couldn't get the measure of his face. Or his clothes, or anything other than the beard greyer than the wild hair, shadowed eyes and strong shoulders, a grainy figure against the black shore like an old photo. He didn't move, and she relaxed a little at that. Enough to answer.

'I came back, yes. I didn't go out far.' She tried a smile, felt her scars stretch and gave up. 'I didn't see you. Sorry, are you walking?'

The man canted his head very slightly. A wave broke in a single, percussive beat; Tinna wanted more than anything to walk away, towards drugs and warmth and stillness.

'Ertu týndur?' he said.

She almost laughed. Was she lost? 'Yes,' she said before she could stop herself. 'No. I mean…' she hesitated, then switched to Icelandic. 'I'm staying here. Do you know Lilith?'

A flash of teeth in the beard, two waves broke over one another in a cruciform of white against the blue-black sea. 'We know one another, Lilith and I. You're the granddaughter then, of the last to drown. You came back.'

'What?' she said. *The last to drown.* But the sky behind him was shifting from dove grey to granite and she was too sore and too cold to stand here making polite conversation with a stranger. 'I'm…' but she could not find the Icelandic for *recovering* or *healing* and they weren't entirely true anyway, 'I was ill. I'm here to get better. And actually, sorry, but I have to rest now.' She tried to take a step, but her leg buckled and she stumbled, the sand slipping sly and black beneath her. The man did not move and she was grateful. The pain was a blaze and she was more tired now than she had been for an age. Perhaps, she thought, I will sleep tonight without dreaming of lullabies or ghosts. Perhaps she would sleep without drowning.

'Hefur þú misst?' he said quietly.

Are you lost, she thought. No. *Have you lost? Have you lost someone?*

'Yes,' she whispered, then louder, 'Goodbye.' Making her cautious way up the bank into the grass, the house ahead of her low and quiet and pale.

Behind her the beach murmured to the tide and all around the air was sharp with cold and her own broken nerve endings.

Lilith didn't notice the missing kayak when she got home. Too busy unloading shopping in the kitchen, talking to the cat in low, half-impatient murmurs as Tinna dragged herself out of a half-dozing nowhere. The threatening snow had arrived, she realised, meaning to join Lilith in the kitchen but instead drawn to the window. It was not heavy but was enough to turn the air phantasmagorical and shrink the horizon down below the mountain peaks and in from the sea. What would it be like, she thought, to be out on the sea in the snow? There was something magical about the thought somehow.

'It won't last,' Lilith said from behind her. 'How are you feeling?'

Tinna flexed her right hand. 'Do you know the fisherman who passes each day?' Because it had just now occurred to her who the man on the beach might have been. Why his silhouette had looked very slightly familiar.

She watched the snow fall over the water, a million precious things undone. It took her a while to realise she'd asked a question and Lilith had not answered. 'Lilith?' she said, turning, her left hand on the windowsill to hold herself steady. The room swayed around her just like the sea had done earlier.

'That's likely Árni Leifsson from Arnastapi,' her aunt said. The lines bracketing her mouth had deepened, the way Tinna's mother's did when she was fighting her own self.

Tinna nodded. It was likely Árni Leifsson from Arnastapi, who of course would know about her, and about her grandmother. She turned back to the window, the susurrate silence of the snowfall slipping inside like a cat, and wondered whether she had the energy to ask.

'Red boat, yes?' Lilith said into the quiet.

Tinna pressed her right hand against the glass, then tipped forward until her forehead rested there too. Her entire vision was filled with the shifting maze of the snow, and the drugs swam through her like silk, like serpents.

'Tinna. The boat was red, yes?'

She blinked. 'Maybe,' she said. Red or black, fresh blood or old, love or death. They were all the same thing.

'Does that mean yes?'

The wind blew a rush of snow against the window and Tinna started, turned back to her aunt, hearing the tone of her voice finally. What did it matter, she thought, whether it was Árni in his red boat or some other man in his black one? 'No,' she said slowly. 'It was black. Unless it was the light, I guess.'

'The light,' Lilith said. 'Yes, yes, it was likely that.' But she was staring at Tinna as though she wished to peel away her surface and discover a different answer.

They've already done that, Tinna wanted to say, and they failed. She opened her mouth to say that she had spoken to him, to ask whether it was true her grandmother had drowned and was *that* what was beneath Lilith's fear. Not Tinna's own fallibility but a simple dread of the water.

But Lilith had left the room before she could brace herself for the inevitable refusal to answer.

Chapter Four

She woke barely an hour after falling asleep that night. The book of folktales fallen shut on the blanket beside her, and when she turned her head there was a blur of movement at the window.

Just the snow, she thought. Just the snow falling along a thousand million different pathways and for one single moment looking like a face.

Lilith must have gone to bed because the house was quiet. Only the hushed voices of the snowflakes and the sea, and Tinna's own heartbeat to mark the movement of the world. She wouldn't be going back to sleep anytime soon.

So instead she pulled herself upright, bracing for pain and weighing it as it stirred. A walk, she thought. A walk through the snow in the dark, how good that would be. How peaceful and perfectly cut off from reality. Not quite a wonderland but perhaps a kind of homeland instead. She remembered Lilith telling her to walk around the house, and could feel nothing but a distant pity for her aunt, for understanding so little and for fearing the sea so much.

The snow and the cold hit her like a thousand tiny burns on the skin of her face and neck. She had put boots on this time, and Lilith's coat and her cane, but her hands and head were bare. The cold was welcome though, and she turned almost eagerly towards the shore, wanting to watch the snow land on the black waves more than she wanted to worry about her aunt's worry. There had been enough of other people's concern weighing down on her since she first woke in the hospital, she could at least be free of them here in the dark.

The tide was low so she climbed carefully over boulders and grass and walked down the long shore to the water, slipping over slick pebbles that were so black in the starless blackness that it felt like there was nothing there at all, each step a leaping off into the unknown. The snow nestled into her hair and the collar of the coat, a stinging reminder that she was awake. Which was good, she thought; it was good to be sure of that sometimes. The waves had picked up since that morning, pulling back and then folding over on the slope of the beach with long rolling hisses. She stood just out of reach of it, watching the glimmer of white on the cresting water, the way the falling snow simply vanished into darkness when it reached the sea.

Vini mínum vagga ég í ró
En úti biður andlit á glugga

She had been waiting for it, she realised. The last time she'd been down here in the dark, the sea had sung her a lullaby and brought a face to her window. She'd come down here to see if any of it was real, or no, of course it wasn't real, but to see how deeply her shattered mind was tangled. And here it was again, the sea singing a lullaby, the black sky shedding white snow, the black sea swallowing it and her in between it all, humming a tune she had never known.

Vini mínum vagga ég í ró
En úti biður andlit á glugga

She waited. The sea hissed and shivered.

'What's the rest of it?' she asked. Whether some damaged recess of her mind or the sea, she didn't much care. What difference did it make where the answers came from, as long as they came.

Vini mínum vagga ég í ró

'I know,' she whispered. 'What else?'

En úti biður andlit á glugga

'Tell me,' she whispered, leaning heavily on her cane and lowering to a crouch, pain branching up her leg, leaving pathways so bright they shone in her mind like lightning. 'Tell me,' she said to the sea. 'If I can remember a lullaby I'd forgotten I even knew, then I can remember the rest. Give him back to me.'

She waited, testing the gaps in her mind for whispers like you might test a wound to see if it was still bleeding.

'Give him back to me.'

She startled. A wave broke like a ribbon all along the shore, the snow fell into it and died.

'Give her back to me.'

Tinna lifted her left hand to her mouth and pressed cold fingers to her cold lips, tasted salt and ice.

'Give her back to me.'

Her mouth had not moved. That soft voice murmuring echoes of her thoughts; it was not her. Or it was, but it was all in her mind. Auditory hallucinations, she thought. That's what the neurologist would say; it's what she *did* say, Tinna remembered now.

You must expect some challenging psychological side-effects while your nerves heal. Your senses and memories might be stimulated seemingly at random as synapses re-establish connections.

How long will it take?

That's hard to say. You might have hallucinations, auditory or visual, even olfactory. You may have particularly vivid and disturbing dreams. You might experience 'brain fog', cognitive dysfunction; you might suffer waking nightmares—what we call night terrors in children.

How can I remember?

You can't force it. If you are troubled by these symptoms, or feel that they are getting worse rather than better, phone my secretary and we'll see you a little sooner than scheduled. Okay?

'Give her back to me.'

The snow settled on Tinna's fingers, her cheeks, her eyelashes; a wave lapped at her boots and she rose slowly to standing, pain climbing then settling again like the water, and wrapped her right hand over her left on the cane handle, her fingers around her wrist, pulse beating blindly beneath her thumb.

'Enough,' she whispered, and turned away. Whatever it was she had hoped to find here, she had failed.

Someone sighed. Just as they had in the graveyard, and in her dreams. A sigh full of endings, and some formless thing lurched within her. Was this a memory like the lullaby must be a memory? Was it him sighing or her, was it his last, oh god was it his last? And had he known, and had he known she was there, and had he gone gently and would it be easier to bear if he had?

If she knew these things, if she knew whether she had greeted him with a kiss, whether they had argued or laughed or not spoken at all… If she knew these things then surely it would all be a little easier to bear.

Her mother had told her not to try.

There are some things it's best not to know, Tinna. Believe me, I know what I'm talking about. Sometimes you just have to say 'No, digging into this won't change anything and is only going to get me hurt', and you walk away and don't look back. Do you hear? You walk away from it, Tinna, because there are worse things than forgetting.

What could possibly be worse than forgetting?

But her mother hadn't replied, only huffed out an impatient breath and drained the last of her coffee, setting it back on the table heavily. They had sat there in Tinna's lounge in complex silence, both of them reading or her mother reading and her drifting into sleep. Conversations with her mother were always like that. Staccato and ending at odd moments like an undescended chord. And now Tinna was at the house, standing on Lilith's doorstep with her own footprints and the points of the cane leading back to the sea even though she couldn't remember walking here, a miniature drift lying against the threshold that collapsed on itself when she pushed the door open.

She saw the light in the lounge through the frosted boot room door, but gave it no thought until she was shed of boots and coat and came into the hall. The cat was sitting at the point where the hall opened into the lounge and it was only seeing it there, backlit and green-eyed, that she realised.

'Hello Lilith,' she said. There was movement out of sight, a rustle that sounded like the curtains resettling. The cat blinked slowly. 'Hello cat,' she added. Her right hand was no warmer than it had been and she wondered at the wisdom of placing it against a radiator. What were the inclinations of chilblains anyway, the gradients of cold and heat that made warming harmful rather than healing?

'Köttur,' Lilith said, coming into view. 'His name is Köttur.'

'Cat?' Tinna found herself smiling, the movement crackling against her cold skin, her burning scars. 'He's called Cat?'

Köttur looked up at them both, raised a grey paw and began to wash his face. Lilith turned back into the lounge. She was in pyjamas, Tinna realised, her pale feet bare, her hair for once not perfectly tamed. There was something Tinna ought to say, an apology at least, but just then, rubbing her left fingers over the lifeless skin of her right hand, she couldn't bring herself to speak. Why was Lilith owed an apology simply because Tinna had walked down to the water? If the world owed Tinna no penance, then she, surely, owed her aunt no blind obedience. She went into the kitchen and filled the kettle, the bright light reflecting off the counters and windows, making the world beyond into something imagined. Perhaps it was, Tinna thought, perhaps she had built all of it from the abyss within her own mind—the black sea swallowing the silent snow, the lullaby and the deadly cold.

No. No, some of it at least was real. The snow sucking the heat from her hand, the black sand on the hems of her pyjamas, the sense of being suspended between two realities, between remembering and drowning.

Give her back to me. So strange that she'd shifted her own words like that.

'What did you say?'

She turned, startled, the kettle clicked off and Lilith was standing two paces away, her eyes narrow and shadowy.

'I didn't…' she faltered. Her left hand was warming now; she rubbed again at her right and thought for a moment that she could feel it ache. A pulse of weighty pain in the bones of her palm, there and gone. Steam roiled and unwound against the ceiling and Tinna's head spun.

'Give her back to me. You said, *Give her back to me.* Why?'

'No,' Tinna whispered. Pain spun along her bones like a dancer. 'No. Give him back. I said…' She frowned. She was thawing out and with the warmth came a tide of exhaustion, of pain and muffled bewilderment like fog. 'It doesn't matter,' she whispered.

Lilith came forward and made tea with short, sharp movements. 'It does,' she said flatly. 'I woke and you were gone. I was just about to go looking for you but saw you coming back… you were on the beach.' She paused, holding the teabag over the bin, her arms flexed and she let the lid drop with a clang. 'People who wander around the moors and the beaches of Iceland at night remain outside, Tinna. This country is not kind to the lost or the—' she cut off abruptly.

'Foolish,' Tinna finished for her, nodding slowly, the movement too big and too graceless, drunk on fatigue. There had been flowers in the bin, she realised. The blue ones from the windowsill that she'd put into a glass. It felt like a slap.

'Yes, the foolish.'

The snow whickered against the dark window, laying itself along the sill like a promise. Or a threat, Tinna thought. 'I've survived worse,' she said, and in her own mind she wasn't talking about the sea or the mapless dark, she was talking about the woman in front of her, the rigid distance and blank walls, the sheer inescapable familiarity of being shut out.

Lilith sighed, then shook her head once. 'Come on,' she said, a hand on Tinna's arm visible but unfelt, and then Tinna was sitting down with a pyrotechnic flare of agony on her bed. The cat, Köttur, jumped up beside her, gave her one sceptical glance then lay down with a hefty sigh. Lilith crouched in front of her and for a moment she could have been any one of a dozen hospital porters, nurses, auxiliaries, their calm faces and calm voices finding a way through the blank spaces within her; the static of the pain. 'Sleep, Tinna. You look…'

Yes, Tinna wanted to say, there is no word for it, is there? Not really, not if you are too frightened to say *broken*.

'You are not broken,' Lilith said, her voice sharp enough to cut. 'Don't talk nonsense. You are scarred and grieving. That's it.'

Tinna shook her head mutely.

'You have to let it go,' Lilith said quietly, and this too cut through the pain, more effectively than her sharpness had done.

'No,' Tinna said simply.

Lilith stared at her, then pushed to her feet. Köttur opened both eyes, contemplated waking, then stretched a paw and returned to sleep. Tinna wondered if perhaps her dead nerves would heal by the brushing of that misty grey fur the way they had not done to pinpricks or massage or the icy sea. It seemed as likely as anything did.

'I'm sorry, but there's no going back, Tinna. If you don't let him go then you are condemning yourself, and who knows who else. You have to be more than your grief, otherwise that is all you will ever be. Forever. Is that what you want?'

Want? Tinna thought. Too distracted by that to dwell on the sheer hypocrisy. She rested her right hand experimentally on the cat's flank, he twitched an ear but did not stir and she stroked lightly for fear of pressing too hard. Nothing. Pain wrapped its tentacles around her spine, her skull, her jaw; her leg spasmed then stilled. A gust of wind cast snow against the window like a handful of rice and confetti.

'I want to remember,' she said.

'Then rest, heal, don't wander about by the sea in the dark.'

Her aunt's eyes were too like her mother's just then, too sharp and shuttered and full of hidden things.

Tinna sighed. 'Goodnight, Lilith. I'm sorry for waking you.' The hems of her pyjamas were still wet from sea and snow, but she lay down anyway, pulling the duvet over her, arranging her limbs with a care learned from a hundred grim hours. She closed her eyes, the cat leapt off the bed and after another long moment the door closed. She lay listening to the snow whispering against the glass. If it were only about want, and only in her head, then the voice would come to her now, she thought. It would be in the snowfall, whispering lullabies and sorrow. But the night stayed wordless. Because it wasn't just about *wanting*, it was about *being owed*, and it was only the sea that understood.

Chapter Five

'Swimming,' Gerdie said. 'Come on, let's go.'

Tinna stared at the woman standing in the hallway. Lilith had left a note on the kitchen counter saying Gerdie would come around, but Tinna had forgotten all about it until the door opened, the doorbell ringing as an afterthought.

'Do you live here,' she heard herself say. 'Normally, I mean.' She knew, saying it, that it was none of her business but Köttur was wending his way around Gerdie's ankles shedding his fur proprietorially on her thick socks and she felt guilty if it was true. She felt guilty anyway, although she was not entirely sure why. For being where she was not wanted, for returning without her brother; for being the one who survived.

Gerdie tipped her head sideways, assessing her like a morsel, and then smiled. 'No,' she said. 'We're too used to our own space for that. But it's semantics, most of the time.'

Tinna looked down at Köttur, the room shifted from dove grey to slate and snow began to whisper against the window again. She wasn't sure when it had stopped but she had woken to a still and monochrome world, all black sea, black cliffs and the fragile white flatlands caught between the two like a blade in a fist.

'Swimming,' Gerdie repeated and Tinna realised she had not answered, or moved. She looked up now, met the other woman's sharp, patient gaze.

'You don't have to stay away because of me,' she said eventually, lifting her right hand to gesture meaninglessly at the house, Lilith's bedroom, the life that was theirs.

Gerdie smiled again. 'Don't fret, I'm not so easily scared off. But I think Lili needs to spend time with you. It'll do her good.' She clapped her hands together, and Tinna started slightly at the sound. 'Now. I have a spare costume in case you didn't bring one. I'll grab a towel, you grab anything else you need. We go into Stykkishólmur; the school don't use it on Tuesdays so we'll not be inundated. They've two hot pools that I think you'll like. Good for healing.'

Tinna lifted her left hand to touch her face, thinking that anyone who thought those scars were going to heal was fooling themselves.

'Your leg, I was thinking of,' Gerdie said, and Tinna dropped her hand again. Gerdie moved past her towards the bathroom, and Köttur returned to the lounge without a glance at Tinna.

'What did you mean *It'll do her good*,' Tinna said slowly. 'What did…' she trailed off. Some half-formed heartache drifting through her and away again. Her aunt and her mother, and a man saying calmly, *You're the granddaughter then, of the last to drown*. She thought of the sea, the lullaby, the pure recognition of hurt and anger and woundedness, and shook her head as if that might clear it.

Gerdie had a hulking, well-weathered truck and Tinna's leg threatened to give way beneath her as she climbed into the passenger seat. She saw Gerdie glance down to check her seat belt and thought that she must be a mother, to do that. A raven watched them from the churchyard wall and snow was gathering against the graves like the hems of bridal gowns and Tinna looked away from both. Lilith had come to her wedding but slipped away without saying goodbye. Tinna rubbed the fingers of her left hand over the cold cotton of her jeans, thinking of ravens and white lace and the look on his face when he had turned to her at the altar. Elías whispering as he walked her up the aisle, *You two are going to be so happy.*

'She misses you all.'

Tinna blinked. Snow was swept across the windshield with a wet hush, the passage of other cars on the road marked out by black lines in the white. It occurred to Tinna that she would have been nervous, driving even in this light fall, and that this if nothing else marked her as an outsider now. It occurred to her that she might never drive again. *Not advisable*, the doctor had said, and she had not bothered to ask whether that was because of the drugs, the amnesia or the nerve damage. Thank god, she thought, that it had been him driving and not her. How would you ever reconcile yourself to that? Instead she had only to reconcile this, *How dare the world take him, and how dare the world take her memory of him?* And sometimes fleetingly, guiltily, *How dare he? How dare he make such a mistake and take* himself *away from her?* Although she didn't know if he had made a mistake. She didn't remember. How dare the universe contain moments of such random cruelty, how dare it make anything irrevocable, even death?

'She's glad you're here.'

Tinna looked away from the cruel, snow-filled shapes of a lava field and all the anger that had nowhere to go made her throat ache. The scars on her face burned like half a dozen fires.

'Did she come to the funeral?' she said quietly. She thought she knew the answer, but was not certain.

Gerdie changed gear, turned onto a road away from the cliffs, towards the scattered edges of a town. 'She wanted to.' She made a soft sound and added, 'That's a useless thing to say, isn't it? No, you're right, she didn't.'

It hurt. It ought not have, but it did.

She remembered his mother weeping silently, folding Tinna into a vast embrace and rocking her like a child. *I am thankful he had you*, she had whispered into Tinna's hair. *I am thankful that my boy was so loved. And I know he is glad that you survived; he will rest easier knowing you are safe.*

Tinna had pulled back and stared bewildered into her dark, red-rimmed eyes, searching for the lie, the resentment, and not finding it.

Tinna, her mother had said. *Time to go.*

Tinna couldn't remember whether she had spoken at all that entire day. Her mind had been all pain and panic and incomprehension, her ribs cracked open and her heart exposed to the air.

'She had her reasons, but that doesn't make it right.'

Tinna frowned at the sky, then remembered. Gerdie swung the truck into a car park, pulled it into a far corner, hesitated and turned it around to park close to the swimming pool doors then reached over the seat for the bags.

'What were they?' Tinna said.

'Pardon?'

Tinna pressed her right hand against the window, felt

nothing at all. 'Her reasons, what were they?'

There was silence in the truck and silence in Tinna's head. She wasn't sure she particularly cared but then there were so many unknowns now and this one at least had the benefit of being old and painless.

'That's for her to tell you, I think,' Gerdie said eventually.

Tinna smiled, felt the scars pull, took her hand from the window and pressed it against her cheek, the cold like electricity. 'If she's anything like Mum, that means I'll never know.'

Gerdie huffed in what might have been laughter. Someone passed in front of the truck and entered the building, behind which, Tinna realised, a ghost of steam was rising. She'd forgotten that the pool would be outside, heated by buried fury, and now she did finally want to swim. To submerge herself in tectonic incandescence just like she wanted to drown herself in oceanic cold.

'They're as alike as you get, that's for certain,' Gerdie said and Tinna thought, yes, perhaps they were. The fury and the numbness, the fire and the ice, they were both endless and all consuming. But then she caught up with the conversation again and looked at her aunt's partner, who appeared to know her mother well enough to know this.

'What do you know?' she whispered.

Gerdie sighed, looked away and then back again. 'Come on,' she said. 'This is a conversation for a hot pool or strong alcohol, and I imagine you aren't allowed the latter.'

She didn't swim, because by the time she had shivered naked through the showers, her leg was spasming so hard she only hobbled gracelessly barefoot over the cool tiles to the hot pools and climbed into them with a gasp at the heat, the scent of sulphur and deep places in the steam. Gasped again at the way the pain shied away from the scalding water, retreating to burrow into her bones. She pressed her right palm flat against the surface of the pool, then let it sink, unfelt. If she were honest she wasn't even sure she wanted to heal, not really, not when it felt too much like leaving him behind.

Gerdie climbing down beside her made her open her eyes.

'You probably should get out and swim for a while. You'll get dizzy if you stay in here too much longer.'

Tinna blinked, straightened from where she had sunk up to her neck. She had not noticed closing her eyes, and had no idea how long she'd been here. There was someone swimming sedate lengths in the pool, and a soft-skinned man walking towards the changing rooms, casting them a brief incurious glance as he passed. From that angle, he could see only the unchanged half of her face. It was nice, sometimes, to only be glanced at and forgotten.

'My leg,' she said, moving it experimentally. There was fine sweat at her hairline as if the clouds above were not ponderous with snow, and Gerdie was almost certainly right. But, 'My leg,' she repeated meaninglessly.

'Helps, does it? Thought it might.' Gerdie straightened her own legs out with a sound of pleasure. 'Now, I promised an answer. Still want it?'

Tinna looked up from the wavering outline of her own limbs to the other woman. An answer? She knew, as soon as she got out of this pool, the pain would reclaim her, then she would take her drugs and the world and her curiosity would recede a little bit. She didn't know whether she wanted to get out of the pool or not.

'What do you remember about leaving here?' Gerdie asked.

Tinna frowned. 'Did you know us then? Did we meet?'

Gerdie tipped her head from side to side. Where her hair was wet at the nape of her neck, it was curling darkly. 'I was living away then but came back a couple of times in the year before you left. The last time I was pregnant with my eldest daughter, it was… a strange visit.'

'Because of you and Lilith?'

Gerdie smiled slightly. 'No. Well, yes maybe. But mostly because I'd known Jóhanna and Lilith for years and they were almost unrecognisable.'

She shifted, Tinna lifted her right hand out of the water, watched steam rise from it like it was alive.

'How?' she said when she realised Gerdie was not going to carry on.

Gerdie shifted her weight again, bent her legs up and leaned forward onto her submerged knees, her chin almost in the water. Tinna suspected that it was unlike her to fidget; she suspected that if her drugs were not wearing off and her leg for once not hurting, she'd not have noticed.

'That was a month before your mother left. The time before was when I came back for your grandmother's funeral.' She heaved in a breath, almost inhaling water, her gaze on something Tinna could neither see nor remember. 'They were barely speaking and yet clinging together like… like those monkeys do, you know? They'd been close before, but this was…' She shrugged. 'At first I thought it was just about the house, and grief. It's a difficult thing, to pack up your parent's things, emotionally bruising.'

Tinna thought of her own flat, all the empty spaces within

it, how she had walked gingerly through the rooms in the dark unable to bear it and unable to leave. 'Mum said that was why we left. Because she wanted to sell the house and Lilith wouldn't.'

'Did you believe her?'

'I don't—' The sweat at her hairline was cold in the cold air, her skin hot, black stars beginning to float across her vision. She tipped her head back to the waiting sky and wished for snow. 'I never know with her. She's very reserved.'

'Secretive?'

She huffed out a ghost of a laugh. 'Yes. Yes, that.'

The first time Tinna had met his mother, she had taken Tinna's hand and grinned. *Come sit with me, let me tell you all the embarrassing stories about Benjamin I can remember.* He had laughed and kissed his mother's cheek. *You can't scare me*, he'd said, *Tinna knows all my secrets already.*

'We should get out. You're going pale and I can't have you fainting on me.' There was a splash and flurry of water, but Tinna didn't turn her head from the clouds, remembering, waiting.

'What is the secret?' she heard herself say. What was the secret? It felt like a much more vast question than just why two sisters had become estranged. It stretched out from her to the lullaby at the shoreline, the face, the half-remembered sigh, all the missing minutes and hours hidden within her own mind.

'I don't know,' Gerdie said.

Of course, Tinna thought. Of course not.

'All I know is that they were both very, very afraid after their mother's death. And *that* was why Jóhanna left, and that is why Lilith doesn't want you wandering around at night.'

Tinna tore her eyes away from the clouds and stared at

Gerdie. Her cheeks were pink with heat and her eyes were sad.

'I thought my grandmother drowned. Why would that frighten Mum enough to make her leave?'

Gerdie shook her head. 'She did drown. But it wasn't just a… a fear of accidents, it was more.' Her gaze slipped from Tinna's eyes to her scars and back again. 'They were terrified. And Jóhanna had you and your brother to protect. If not for you two she would never have left Lilith like that.'

'Like…'

'In danger.'

'In…' Tinna frowned, felt her skin pull and ache. The black stars swam slow labyrinths across her vision and she needed her drugs, she thought, she needed a cool drink and the simplicity of pain.

Gerdie was not looking at her now. 'Lilith has never said and I've given up asking. But after their mother died they were both convinced that you were all in danger.'

Tinna blinked. Darkness drifted through her, around her, in all the blank spaces of her body. 'From what?'

'Come on. Out you get.' Gerdie's hand was on her left arm, her grip unapologetic and firm. Tinna went unresisting, the water and its heat washing off her like blood and the cold catching her up. She wavered. Someone called a question and Gerdie called back, the Icelandic too rapid for Tinna to parse.

'Sorry,' Gerdie said more quietly. 'I talked too long. Lost track. Careful now. I've water in the changing room.'

Gerdie guided her as inexorably and smoothly as a nurse and Tinna obeyed the way she had done with them. Her right leg was numb and unsure of itself, and she did not especially want to be walking at all. She wanted to sleep, to lay herself down in a blanket of snow and sleep until the stars rose and the sea rose and she could, perhaps, dream of the forgotten.

- *How you doing?* Elías had sent while she was in the pool. And, when she had not replied,

    - *Seen any auroras yet?* And then,

    - *Spoken to mum? She rang asking if I could persuade you to come home. I'm in disgrace for taking you to the airport.*

Tinna sat on the bench in the changing room while Gerdie packed their bags and typed out a slow reply. There was a young mum and her toddler stripping for the showers, the toddler stared, the mother didn't.

    - *So apparently we left because mum was frightened of something. Any idea what?*

He replied immediately, as if he had been waiting. - *What? Who said that? Lilith?*

    - *Her partner Gerdie. Do you remember our grandmother? I don't.*

    - *A bit. She was quiet and a bit dreamy, used to tell us stories but didn't leave the house much. I think she wasn't well. Why?*

Tinna tried to call up memory of this woman—surely a five year old would have enough memories of a grandparent for at least the sense of them to last. But all she remembered of Iceland was the colours and the cold, the feel of pebbles within her palm, chasing after her brother along the shore.

    - *She drowned. Lilith is still really frightened of the sea. I wondered.*

    - *You'd think she'd have been happy to move then!*

'Ready?' Gerdie said, and Tinna looked up almost guiltily. The showers were running, the child giggled and it echoed oddly off the bone-white tiles.

'Yes,' she said, and rose carefully. Once in the truck, she replied, not picking through her words for coherence the way she normally did, too aware of Gerdie and too somnolent.

- I know why she stayed. The sea understands loss. But I don't understand why she'd fear it, unless it's not the sea she fears but being the one who survived.

Then she put her phone away and watched the town slip away, the road hurl itself into the mountains as if that weren't an act of unrelenting faith.

Chapter Six

Her mother rang that evening as Gerdie and Lilith were cooking in the kitchen, the radio on and their voices soft and muffled. The drugs and the lingering traces of the hot pool were lying heavily in Tinna's bones, stranding her on the sofa with nothing in her mind or in her blood other than the sound of the sea beyond the window and the ceaseless awareness of the missing.

'How are you getting on?'

'Fine,' Tinna said, her voice rusty as if she had not spoken for weeks.

'How's your hand? Any change?'

'No.' She closed her eyes. 'There might not be.'

A short silence. She could guess at the frown lines on her mother's face. 'Well, early days, they said. Didn't they? We don't know anything for sure yet.'

Other than that he is gone, Tinna thought. He is gone and I am here. She did not say it. The drugs made the thought into something almost unreal; the travesty far stronger than the pain.

'Lilith is well, I assume.'

Tinna listened to the lack of question, the closed full stop.

Gerdie laughed in the kitchen. 'She's being very kind,' she said slowly.

'Good. Look, I was thinking. She's working and you're out on your own there. I found a hotel in Reykjavík that has a spa pool and a museum, and is right next to cafés and The Pearl so you'd have things to do, and the pool would be good for you. I thought I could pay for you to stay for a few days. As a treat. Lilith could take you on her way to work tomorrow. Shall I book it now?'

The sky through the window was as translucent and fragile as a sliver of shell, and Tinna could almost feel the great weight of space pressing against the world like a fist.

'No, I'm okay here, and Gerdie is—'

'I think you should go. Just for a few days. It would give Lilith and Gerdie a break.'

Tinna flinched very slightly; a flock of shorebirds rose up into the air, whirled once and were gone in a flicker of silver. 'I've only just arrived. Maybe next week, Mum. It's kind of you to offer.'

Her mother didn't answer, and Tinna breathed through a wave of pain, shifting her weight to ease it. She realised slowly that it perhaps was not kindness at all. *They were both convinced that you were all in danger.*

'Mum, what happened to our grandmother?' she said before she could think better of it.

Silence. The sea beat against the shore like a heart. The radio burst into song.

'Nothing happened. She died. Have you spoken to your brother?'

'Yes, but—'

'They've rebooked their holiday, did he say? They're off next week for the Easter break.'

He'd cancelled a holiday in October, when she had been too often unconscious to tell him not to. Later she'd said, *You should have gone. No reason to miss out just because—*

Because my sister is critically ill in hospital and has just lost her husband? Getting a bit of sunshine and beach is more important than that?

He'd sounded angrier than he'd been in years and at her wide eyes, he had sighed and run a hand roughly over his face.

I know we don't have the best track record at sticking around, this family. But that doesn't make it right, Tinna. That doesn't make it okay.

She hadn't understood what he meant at the time, but she did now.

And she had not yet replied to his last message. Perhaps she ought to tell him, if she could find the words.

'Tinna? Are you still awake?'

She lifted her right hand, the one not holding the phone, touched her eyes, her scarred cheek. 'Yes,' she said. 'Mum…'

'What is it?'

That doesn't make it okay.

'Why did we leave here?'

'What's she said?' Her mother's voice was sharp, icy, and Tinna recognised that tone well. There was more than one way of absenting yourself. Her mother knew them all.

'Nothing. Just…' The effort that this required felt monumental, like each word, and each of her mother's words, were links in an iron chain around her chest. 'Someone said you took us away for our safety. Was it… was it our father?'

A short, hard laugh. 'Him? That useless lump of

chickenfeed couldn't threaten a vole. Whoever said that clearly never met him, more luck them. No, Tinna. Don't listen to any nonsense.'

'So what—'

'Right, better go anyway. Think about the hotel, let me know tomorrow and I'll book it. I think you should go, I really do. Give my best to Lilith.'

'Mum.'

'Bye, Tinna. Look after yourself. Bye.'

Tinna lowered the phone into her lap, studied the screen and thought that it did not matter how familiar the pattern of a parent's rejection was, it would never cease to hurt.

She does love us, Ben, she'd said to him once, drinking the last of her wine after her mother had been for dinner.

Yes, he'd said. *But she doesn't let you close, does she? Why is that?*

I don't know. It's just the way she is.

Lilith has never said and I've given up asking, Gerdie had said.

Pain flickered across the back of her skull, down the length of her spine to burst against the bones of her pelvis like fireworks. She had probably been motionless too long and needed to get up, to walk the nerves into some form of quiescence again.

Don't listen to any nonsense. What was the nonsense, Tinna wondered hazily, that her mum didn't want her to listen to? And if it was nonsense why did she want Tinna to leave? She'd lived for twenty years with her mother's remoteness and her aunt's absence. So it hardly mattered now; only she was *here* now, half-belonging to this strange land the way she was half-belonging to herself. The sea like a companion and her aunt's fear like a cage.

'Gerdie said the heat helped,' Lilith said when they were eating. Tinna was not so much eating as remembering, occasionally, to try.

'Yes,' she said, then to Gerdie, 'Did I thank you? I can't remember if I said thank you.'

Gerdie's eyes were measuring, not unkindly but the way people did with someone like her, she'd learned. Weighing the distance between health and illness, between compassion and pity. 'You're welcome. Next time we'll make sure you don't stay in so long. That was my fault.'

'No,' Tinna said. 'No, it wasn't.'

'Do you have trouble sleeping?'

Lilith stilled, fork suspended, and Tinna almost smiled. She didn't mind the question, it was only that there was no answer that didn't lead to other, much harder questions.

I'm outside, are you coming?

I'm coming.

'Yes,' she said, and then honestly, 'Because it's harder at night.'

Gerdie nodded. 'It is, that's true.'

Tinna wondered. She wondered about the father of Gerdie's daughters and the death of her own grandmother and the way that death had shifted an entire world. Perhaps all deaths did that. Knocked the world off its axis, sent it spinning along a different trajectory through the unknown universe.

'Is that why you walk?' Lilith said.

Tinna could feel it already, the pull of the darkness outside, the sing-song susurration of the sea. He was there in her mind like a lodestone and sometimes there was no looking away, there was only giving yourself the space to look, and to fall apart. 'Yes,' she said. 'And walking helps the pain.' Until it didn't.

Lilith nodded, studied her half-empty plate with her face tight and blank. 'If you have to, then walk inland. Up past the church along the road. I'll leave a torch out but there's little enough traffic at night.'

No, Tinna thought. That would not do. There was no comfort in an empty road, not like there was in the sea.

'So,' Gerdie said and Tinna realised that they had been silent for too long. That she had not replied and Lilith had not looked away from her. 'So, hot pool as often as possible. And small walks in between. We can manage that easily enough.'

'Tinna?'

Tinna blinked, realised her gaze had drifted to the window. 'Yes,' she said, not really caring what she was agreeing to, only wanting to be able to stop talking.

'I've a couple of walkers' maps at home. I'll bring them over tomorrow.'

'Are there…' Tinna frowned, pressed her right hand into the aching muscle of her thigh. 'Are there boats going out? That fisherman who's out there every morning, could I go out with him? I'd like to…' be flotsam over the deep depths, the deadly-deep, '…go out.'

'Go out with Árni Leifsson?' Lilith looked surprised and faintly disapproving, but differently this time, like she was thinking only of fish scales and engine oil rather than whatever it was that she feared so much. 'I could ask, I suppose. Although you might—'

'It can't be Árni,' Gerdie said. 'He's away all this week. Off to his brother up north. Fiftieth birthday or something.'

'No,' Lilith said. 'He was out yesterday.'

'And this morning,' Tinna added. 'I met him on the beach.' And saying it she remembered his stillness, his words, and reconsidered. There were still things you could lose, she thought, even when you felt like there weren't.

'Well as I've been feeding his idiotic chickens, I'm pretty sure he's away.'

'*No!*' Lilith said again, urgently, crackling. 'Oh no.' She pushed back from the table so hard the chair tipped and fell, her glass on the table edge tipped and fell. Tinna watched it as if it were happening underwater—the glass falling to the hard floor, shattering loudly even as Lilith reached for it, Gerdie jumping to her feet.

Tinna did not move.

She listened to the glass breaking, the chair crashing. Lilith swearing sharply and Gerdie saying something and the scrabble of claws on wood as the cat fled.

The glass shattering was all high notes and edges. She waited.

'Christ. Sorry. Stay still Gerd, you'll cut your feet.' Then more in Icelandic, rapid movements, the chair righted.

Tinna waited.

'You alright?' Gerdie said. Lilith was on her knees with a dustpan; there was a neat pile of pieces of wine glass on the table, reflecting the ceiling lights like so many fireflies.

'Tinna, are you okay?'

There was nothing there. Tinna sighed, pressed her left hand over her right, squeezing until she could feel the parameters of each bone. She had been covered in tiny cuts almost healed by the time she was awake for long enough to notice anything at all. A nurse had seen her studying her own arm, all the red lines like glyphs.

Broken glass, she'd said, *Some from the accident and some from the firemen getting you out.* She'd stepped forward and turned Tinna's arm over then back again. *Healed up nicely, and none of them very big. You don't remember?*

'Yes,' she said to Gerdie. Lilith straightened, her eyes dark and blank. 'Yes, I'm fine.'

Gerdie and Lilith settled on the sofa with glasses of wine as gold as a sunset, but Tinna couldn't sit. She went to the window and pushed the curtain aside, standing so that her own silhouette made the outside visible, a human-shaped gateway to the dark. It wasn't snowing now, and the sky was clear, a gallows moon hung low over the sea, casting a knife-thin line across the water towards them.

'Now, Lil,' Gerdie said behind her, in a voice that Tinna hadn't heard from her before. 'What's going on, ástin mín? You need to tell us.'

Tinna met her own eyes in the glass.

'Gerdie.'

'What? Hasn't it been long enough?'

'Gerd.'

The silver trail of moonlight vanished, then reappeared as if… Tinna blinked, frowned.

'Twenty some years, Lilith, this thing has hung over you.'

'Twenty some years you've known well enough I don't wish to talk about it.'

…as if someone had passed in front of it, Tinna thought.

She shifted her weight, pain crackling in her leg and hip like barbed wire wrapping around her bones. She leaned her forehead against the glass, her breath on the window forming her own ghost and for a moment the sheer sorrow of it all was too heavy to bear.

'Which would be fine enough if it weren't affecting you so much.'

'It's not—'

'What was that then?' Gerdie was surely gesturing to the dining table, the swept floor. The moonlight vanished again, a heartbeat, reappeared. The barbed wire twisted and Tinna hissed a breath. She was, she realised, waiting for Lilith to get up and walk away.

Someone sighed. Tinna recoiled away from the glass. The condensation from her breath faded and the sea whispered faintly.

'It doesn't matter,' Lilith said quietly, wearily. 'In another week it won't matter, we just need to stay safe until then.'

Condensation bloomed on the window.

Faded. Bloomed again.

Tinna watched it.

It's the drugs, she thought, or the coming frost.

Another cloud of condensation formed and faded on the other side of the glass.

'Listen to yourself, ástin mín. It clearly *does* matter. Who is it you're so afraid of? I guarantee they're no match for me on a bad day.'

Tinna released a held breath and turned very slowly, very carefully, to face the room. Letting the curtain drop, her spine prickling with pain, and something other than pain.

Outside waits a face at the window.

Oh god, she thought.

I'm outside, are you coming?

I'm coming.

'Lilith,' she said. Something in her voice made both women look up at her sharply. Her aunt's face was white and drawn, her shoulders bowed and the cat on her lap wrapped within a cage of her arms.

'What is it?' Lilith said sharply.

But what could she say, and already that terrible, cold moment of watching someone's breath warm the outside of the glass was blurring, becoming shiftless.

'What is it?' Gerdie said.

'There's...' someone outside. Someone waiting for me. Someone who knows what it is to be lost. And just like that the fear of it was gone, and all she could think was that if there was someone who understood how she felt, who missed anyone as much as she was missing him, then she wanted to know who they were. 'I was hoping there'd be an aurora while I was here.'

It was true. It just wasn't the truth.

'Oh, you'll probably get lucky. It's the season for them,' Gerdie said, but her eyes were intent and to avoid them Tinna moved away from the window, heading for the kitchen.

She and Elías had started at their new school in England four days after leaving this house. She remembered her mother dropping them off at the gate, her face grey with exhaustion and tight with a newly familiar anger; she remembered the words of the other children and the teachers flat and bewildering, and then finally the two of them walking back to their unfamiliar house through unfamiliar streets. Searching around each corner for a horizon and not finding it, feeling small and unspeakably lost.

We won't be here long, Elías had said, breaking their silence. *You'll see, we'll be home in a couple of weeks.*

But Tinna had looked at the crowded sky, the relentless street, and thought that there was no way out of this strange place. It was a maze and they were trapped. *Why did we have to go*, she said, for the hundredth time.

I don't know. But it doesn't matter. She and aunt Lilith fought but they're sisters; they'll make up and then she'll take us home.

I don't like it here.

He had shaken his head wordlessly and slung an arm around her shoulder. A bus passed them in a rush of noise and exhaust, and she had known that they were both yearning for the sea, black pebbles and white tidelines and the particular shade of blue that only existed within the curve of a wave.

Mum will take us home, he had repeated. They'd believed it for months, and then it had been safer not to think it at all, and then it hadn't seemed to matter so much after a while. But now she was home, and she was yearning for the sea.

Chapter Seven

Darkness fell late and swiftly, the sky beyond her bedroom window unleashing stars into the void, and Tinna rose silently. She'd been waiting to see whether sleep or the sea would summon her first, but it had never really been in doubt, and she left her bedroom already lighter with relief.

'We'll come with you.'

She turned, dropping her hand from the inner door.

Gerdie and Lilith were standing at the point where the hall opened into the lounge, both still dressed, Köttur in Lilith's arms, his paws up on her shoulder and his tail hanging down, twitching very slightly.

'You were waiting,' she said. It had not been meant accusingly. No, perhaps it had. She leaned her cane against her hip and pressed her left hand to her cheek, wanting to slump against the wall amongst the coats' gathered shadows. She ought to have known this would happen. After the smashed glass and Gerdie's tightly controlled frustration, of course they would do this.

'Yes.' Lilith lifted her chin and the cat's tailed flicked.

Tinna stared at her, then at Gerdie and wondered what they would do if she began simply to scream. Wondered what she herself would do and would she be able to stop. Would she, afterwards, be able to sleep? 'I don't want company,' she said bluntly.

'That's not the point.'

Gerdie glanced at Lilith then back to Tinna. She lifted one shoulder. 'I know you don't. But if you need to walk at night, and Lilith can't tell us why you mustn't, well. This is the only option left.'

They'd argued, Tinna thought. After she'd gone to bed, they'd argued about this and both of them were brittle with it now. She didn't care. The night was pressing against the walls of the house and all she wanted was its darkness and the sea, the vast scarred land and endless ocean black and full of echoes. The one place in the world where she wasn't alone with her desperation.

'It is not though, is it?' she said quietly, curling her hands into fists, feeling the imbalance between the two like the moment of falling. 'It's not the only option at all. This is ridiculous, and I won't… I need this. I'm sorry.' She turned away; the night sighed softly, she felt it reverberate through her like a touch.

She was pulling her boots on one-handed when Lilith spoke.

'He'll kill you.'

Tinna straightened slowly, her hip flaring with pain at the movement and her cane clattering to the floor. Lilith flinched, but Tinna ignored it, her head both swimming and oddly lucid. Like looking through clear water—everything magnified and distorted. Like grief.

'What?' Gerdie was staring at Lilith. Tinna did not say anything at all, waiting. Her left hand on the wall to stop her falling. The sea murmured beyond the door.

'Please.' Lilith's voice was high and rasping; Köttur flexed and leapt from her arms and without him she looked unutterably exposed. 'Please, come in. I'll... I'll explain.'

'He'll kill me,' Tinna repeated, not moving. The face at the window hovered in her mind, lullabies drifting tidal in her ears. I only want the sea, she thought, and what I am owed. Is that too much to ask?

'He'll...' Lilith's hands moved, half lifting as if to reach for Tinna and pull her bodily back into the hall. 'Tinna, let me explain.'

'Tinna,' Gerdie said. Her eyes were bright and resentment swept sharply through Tinna. This was simply the answer to a riddle for her, wasn't it, the opening of a closed box. Whereas to Tinna it was the thing between her and the only peace she had found since waking in the hospital and being told that he was gone.

She wanted to turn her back, open the front door and step out into the night, but her body was pliant with sedatives and it was hard to fight someone else's will like that. So she shucked her boots off again, wordless, and shut the inner door, bitterness increasing with each step away from the dark. Could she not even have this?

Outside waits a face at the window.

I know, she thought. I know. She had found compassion on the shoreline and her mind had given that compassion a voice, a face. A fiction, but maybe she didn't care.

Give her back to me.

Yes, she thought. Lullabies in the dark and the endless hunger for the lost. Give him back to me.

'Pardon?' Gerdie said.

Tinna blinked. They were in the lounge again, one lone

table lamp in the corner rendering the room all gold and shadows. Gerdie was sitting on the sofa and Lilith was standing where Tinna had been earlier, at the window, holding the curtain back just a few inches, her face averted. Tinna lowered herself carefully into a chair, tried to remember what it had been like to move untrammelled by pain, and by the defence against pain.

'Did you say something,' Gerdie asked again, 'about giving something back?'

Lilith shuddered but did not turn from the window. Tinna shook her head.

The only noise within the room was the cat washing its fur; the only sound without was the wind and the sea indistinguishable. Tinna watched her aunt's profile, so full of tension that it was almost regal. So much like her sister's that Tinna found herself speaking without knowing why.

'Mum won't talk of it either.' To Gerdie as much as to Lilith. 'There's a lot she won't talk about, to be honest. Always has been.' Their father, their grandparents, their aunt, Iceland, grief, longing, fear. 'If we try, do you know what she does?'

Gerdie was watching her steadily; Lilith dropped the curtain. Tinna watched her aunt. 'She walks out.'

Lilith's head moved slightly, but she didn't turn.

'When we were children,' Tinna carried on, 'maybe a year after leaving here, my brother lost his temper. He hated our school, hated speaking English all the time, missed home. He demanded answers. Why had we left, why couldn't we go back. Why didn't she care.'

Tinna inhaled jaggedly, her whole body back there in the past, curled in a corner of the sofa, both frightened of and awed by her brother's anger. Crying silently and unseen.

'What did she say?' Gerdie said eventually. Tinna didn't answer, watching her aunt, feeling more like her brother than she ever had before.

Lilith turned, her eyes shadowed, her arms tight around her waist.

'She walked out,' Tinna said. 'She walked out and didn't come back until the next day. We were six and nine, alone all night because we had asked why we couldn't go home.'

Gerdie swore softly in Icelandic. Then again, less softly.

'We stopped asking after that. We stopped speaking Icelandic unless we were alone. We lost our home and most of our mother's heart and I think we deserve to know why.'

Lilith opened her mouth then closed it again. Pain flared down Tinna's flank and she flinched, and perhaps Lilith misinterpreted that because something in her face changed abruptly and she came forward, sinking onto the sofa and bending forward over her knees, her hair hanging around her face softly.

'It is because no-one would believe it,' she said to her hands. 'Better silence than disbelief.'

'Try us,' Gerdie said.

The wind picked up, gusting against the window and breathing down the chimney, ashes circling behind the glass of the stove. It felt like there were claws in Tinna's femur, and if not for this woman she could have been out there, she thought, becoming numb.

'It's the rule for this family,' Lilith said. 'You don't go down to the sea around the Spring Equinox. Hann mun koma. Hann tekur við greiðslu.'

Tinna frowned, pressed her numb right hand against her

aching thigh, struggling to move through both her frustration and a half-forgotten language. 'He—'

'He will come. He will take payment,' Gerdie said, inflectionless. Her eyes on Lilith were wary and patient and eager all at once, but Lilith was not looking at either of them and suddenly Tinna had no patience for anyone at all. Least of all this taut near-stranger denying her the only thing she had *wanted* since she awoke.

'Who will come?' she snapped. 'Who cares if I go down to the water?'

The cat pressed itself against Lilith and she gathered it up into her arms. 'You won't believe,' Lilith repeated bitterly.

Tinna hissed; the claws in her bones were made of acid. 'I've had my skull bolted back together,' she said, her voice too sharp and too loud but she didn't care. 'And half my face rebuilt. I have three whole months of my life I can't remember. I lost the love of my life and the ability to write, and only one of those is coming back. There's not much that's unbelievable to me anymore.' She was shaking. Even mentioning him slantwise was terrible. Her painkillers were in the other room and she almost understood her mother now. The urge to stand and walk away. 'Just tell me the truth. For once. Please.'

Lilith raised her head and met Tinna's eyes. They stared at one another as the wind laughed in the chimney and the ashes stirred. One of them would rise and walk away, Tinna knew. Lilith would not speak and Tinna had been abandoned too many times already. So this time she would be the one to leave. And it would break something already broken, only this time it would not heal. Please, she thought, to her aunt and her absent mother, to the waiting sea, to her own shattered bones.

'Fine then,' Lilith said softly. 'But don't blame me if you

don't believe.'

The air left Tinna's lungs in a rush, and she was a child all over again, full of hope painted as anger. Neither she nor Gerdie spoke, and she wasn't sure she could even if she dared. The cat purred, his eyes lambent and green and Tinna could hear, beneath the wind and the sea, that voice again, singing softly. She wanted the truth, but she didn't know whether there was a truth powerful enough to keep her from the shore.

'It started a hundred years ago. And it's always the equinox, so I never meant you to... but you're here now, so...' Köttur stretched his paws along Lilith's thighs and her hands buried themselves in his smoke-grey fur. She shook her head. 'I'm not telling this well. It's the sjómaður. There was an accident and his child died. He blamed our great-grandfather and he's never forgiven us. He wants blood, the blood of this family. So he'll take you, if you give him a chance.'

Tinna stared into her aunt's face, then the green eyes of the cat, and wondered whether she were dreaming. 'You think,' she said carefully, touching the fingers of her left hand to those of her right. The song whispered distantly, her leg spasmed as if in reply. 'You think a hundred-year-old fisherman will get me if I go out at night?'

Gerdie had not moved, nor blinked. Her eyes wide and startled.

Lilith's hands tightened, the purr cut off. 'I know how it sounds, but people have died, Tinna. Over the last hundred years, on the Spring Equinox, people from this house go down to the sea at night and drown. It was how your grandmother died. I don't want you to be the next.'

'Grandmother drowned.'

'Yes. She was killed by the sjómaður.'

The ashes stirred in the stove; Lilith's chin was tilted at such a familiar angle that Tinna wanted to scream. Gerdie shifted at last and her frown was the most certain thing in the room. 'Which was it? She drowned or she was murdered by a fisherman?'

Lilith looked at her, bleak and unsurprised. 'You don't believe. I told you you wouldn't.'

'I'm just trying to understand what you're saying.' Although that, even to Tinna's clamouring mind, was clearly not true.

'He's a… a fylgjendur. A follower.'

Gerdie's eyebrows rose and she leaned back as though this word had carried greater heft than all the others.

But it didn't. Something pattered against the hidden windows. Perhaps snow, perhaps not, and Tinna shook her head as if that would clear her mind. The pain was granting her no grace though, it never did, and her skull was a maelstrom of nerve endings, all of them transmitting catastrophe and blind frustration. 'A what?'

Gerdie looked from Lilith to her and screwed her mouth up in what might have been either distaste or doubt. 'A kind of draugr, ghost if you like, that haunts a family. She's saying this fisherman has been haunting your family for a century, killing off family members.'

'Taking payment,' Lilith whispered. The cat stopped purring, flicked its ears. The wind died abruptly so that the only sound was their own breathing and the waves breaking along the shore like a heart.

Tinna pressed her numb right hand over her ribs, then dropped it. 'So if I go down to the sea, I'll drown,' she said, the words metallic on her tongue. 'This ghost will drown me.

That's what you've been afraid of.' The fingers of her left hand ran along the bones of her right, knuckle bones and finger bones. Hers but lost. There but gone. She couldn't fathom her own words. '*This* is why we left?'

Lilith looked at her for the first time, chin lifting once more. 'He drowned my mother. I won't let him have you too.'

'You can't really believe that.' Gerdie's voice was gentler than the words, but Lilith stiffened anyway. Her face hardening into an expression Tinna knew very well.

'My mother—'

'I thought you said she'd been down, depressed, anxious. Can't she have—'

'He drowned her. He drowned her sister when she was a child. He'll drown any member of this family who goes down there around the Spring Equinox. We have to stay safe, stay away.'

So that was it? *The last to drown*, the man had said, which made sense now, but if it was local gossip then why had it taken twenty years for the words to be said in this room? And did the locals whisper about ghosts or about bad luck and depression? The latter, Tinna guessed.

She might almost have felt relief at finally having an answer if she were not breathless at the waste of it all. She remembered the silence in the moment after their mum had walked out, Elías's fury and her tears both swallowed up by the quiet sound of the door lock snicking into place. She remembered them sitting on the sofa holding hands in the gathering dark, too afraid to look at one another because that would make it real, it would make their abandonment complete. Lilith and Gerdie were both watching her, and her hands were not entirely steady. Shadows were flexing and unfurling in the corners of the room, and she was so tired suddenly of secrets and silence, of stories that were nothing but excuses for betrayal. Of anything that stood between her and the one thing she needed—winning back her memory.

No, she thought. This might be Lilith's truth, it might even be her mother's. But it was too little and too late, and not nearly enough to keep her from the sea.

She stood up, wavered as the pain ratcheted higher and realised she couldn't go out tonight anyway. Lilith's stories *had* managed to stop her then, just by trapping her until her own body closed the cage. She moved to the window, pushed the curtains aside and pressed her hands against the glass, yearning. The great black eye of the sea watched her back, the path of moonlight its slim pupil and she wanted to rage, but it would only hurt. When she spoke, the echoes of them both were in her voice anyway, the fury and the pain. 'I don't know what Mum told you but I'm not suicidal. I should be, probably, but I'm not.'

'I didn't mean—'

'Please,' Tinna said. 'Enough. I don't...' know what to believe, or care whether any of it is true, or want anything other than the sea's cold, black compassion. 'I need to lie down.'

'Tinna.'

But Tinna ignored her and left the room.

*

Beyond her bedroom window, the mountains reared up against the star-laden sky like a vast, black breaking wave.

Frustration pulsed a counterpoint to her wounded nerves, and she pulled the curtains firmly closed. She'd come here for peace and instead Lilith was… perhaps this was actually what her mother's decision to leave had been. Not her own fear of ghosts and drownings, but her frustration with a sister who would not let her simply grieve.

Chapter Eight

She couldn't go down to the sea that night. But instead she dreamt of someone waiting for her just out of reach, she dreamt of Ben laughing and Ben sleeping and Ben walking beside her along a mountain track, humming softly. She dreamt of a car and headlights on the wet road, Ben humming softly. The car, the headlights, Ben humming softly. She woke.

Dawn was breaking somewhere, through the open curtains the black peaks of the mountains were painted amber. Fulmars wheeled through the high gilding light like flurries of snow, unfalling and Tinna lay there for a long time watching the sun light the bare rock softly, watching the birds not fall. The voice in her head now she was awake was no longer his, nor was it hers. Older, deeper, deeply Icelandic. Lullabies full of waiting.

Perhaps, she thought, if you lived in a landscape of inexorable danger, and had lost your mother to the sea, you were bound to believe that there was some greater force at work than simply… simply what? *She was depressed, anxious*, Gerdie had said. I am not suicidal, Tinna had said, and it was true. But that did not mean she couldn't understand the lure of it. The promise, if you believed, of being reunited; if you disbelieved, of escaping the pain.

She'd closed the curtains last night, she realised.

The fulmars turned arcs across the sky and Tinna lay on her bed, remembering closing the curtains that were now drawn fully back. She sat up slowly, holding her breath against the pain, easing her leg as it spasmed and tightened. Some mornings it had relaxed into a kind of muscle torpor, but not this morning. It felt instead like she had been standing for too long without moving. She studied the window again, and it was no surprise really that even sleeping she was still searching for him. Reaching for her painkillers and the water, she braced herself, already weary, for the day.

'She's gone to work,' Gerdie said when Tinna stepped into the kitchen, her hair still dripping from the shower. She leaned herself against the counter and tried to brush her hair with her right hand, but either the brush slipped from her grip or it missed her hair completely, and once again she remembered the physiotherapist telling her it was okay to feel frustrated. How sometimes progress was so slow as to be easy to miss, but that didn't mean it was not happening. *Get annoyed by all means*, he had said, *as long as you don't stop the exercises, and don't stop trying to master new skills.*

New skills. Like brushing her hair. She sighed and set the brush down on the counter. It was not so much about frustration, she thought, as about being someone he might not recognise.

'Okay,' she said belatedly, then had no idea what to say next.

Gerdie solved the problem for her. 'So last night was odd.'

'Yes,' Tinna said. The car, the wet roads, the voice humming;

the open curtains. She studied the clean counters, then the grey-blue day beyond the window. A thin day, she thought. Thin light and thin winds, and a heart barely holding on.

Gerdie was watching her. 'Coffee?' she said. 'Swimming again this morning?'

'Don't you have to work?' Tinna had no idea what she did, or when, and realised that she'd made no effort to find out anything about this person who was effectively family. Was it the grief to blame, or the pain or the drugs? Perhaps it was simply that if you are circling the black hole of your own unanswered questions, it becomes impossible to look away. 'What do you do?' she said, making herself turn from the window.

Gerdie gave her a small smile. 'Early retirement. I run a couple of holiday homes. Used to be in local government. Education department.'

'Oh,' Tinna said.

Gerdie handed her a coffee she'd not even noticed her making. 'Does your mother believe in this follower too, do you think?'

For a moment the words made no sense at all, and then they did. Last night and Lilith and stories that sounded more like excuses. She trawled her mind for some kind of answer, and was glad Lilith wasn't here to be hurt by it because the anger might have faded but nothing else had. 'No,' she said. 'I think she left because Lilith believed it. Mum's always been uninterested in anything remotely fantastical. Fairy tales, ghost stories, superstition.' She shrugged. 'Wouldn't read us anything like that when we were young. She said it was all nonsense.'

'Hmm.'

'Is that…' Tinna turned the coffee within her hands, hot and numb, numb and hot. 'You think the same?'

Gerdie screwed her face up, took a long sip of her own coffee then gave Tinna another smile. A slanting, disarming one full of wry mischief. 'Well, the Huldufólk are real enough. But draugr? And fylgjendur? I'm more likely to believe—'

'The Huldufólk are… you believe in elves?' Tinna stared at her.

'You used to as well,' Gerdie said.

Tinna's mouth opened but no words came out because suddenly she was remembering.

She remembered leaving gifts out for them with her brother. She remembered the little red and white doors they had set into tiny barrows for their homes. She remembered her mother laughing, hushing them as they walked through a cluster of trees in the evening. *This is the huldufólk's wood, let's not wake them else they might be annoyed.* It was her mother, *her mother*, who had helped them build the fairy houses, her mother who had warned them about wandering too far in winter else the Jólakötturinn steal them away. Who had said, *Don't follow sounds of singing down to the water, or a nøkker will lure you to a watery grave.*

'What?' Gerdie said. 'What is it?'

'Nothing,' Tinna whispered. Only it wasn't nothing. It was a mother who had laughed and told fairy stories and built them a world full of wonder and the wilds.

'It's not that we all think they're *really* real,' Gerdie said, almost defensively, but regaining that wry smile. 'It's just that it seems wiser not to assume they're *not* real.'

Tinna nodded, too caught up in memories of a mother she'd forgotten existed to really listen.

'It's an old land,' Gerdie went on conversationally. 'And it is not kind to people who disrespect it. Perhaps that is why the old ways linger. Scotland is the same, I think, yes?'

Tinna sipped her coffee. It was stronger than she was used to, bitter on her tongue and hot as cinders. 'A bit, I guess. But... Lilith's ghost...'

The amusement faded. 'Indeed. Lilith's ghost.' Gerdie tapped her fingers against her mug, the sound soft in the quiet room. 'Jæja, does it matter? She'll be happier once the equinox is past, which is... two days' time. Can you curb your wanderings till then, do you think?'

But it does matter, part of Tinna was thinking, just as another part was thinking, You're right. None of this matters at all. She shook her head and startled herself when neither of those thoughts were what she spoke aloud. 'Mum wanted me to go to a hotel in Reykjavík for the next few days.'

Gerdie raised her eyebrows.

'She was insistent,' Tinna added, frowning and feeling her scars pull, remembering a mother who told fairy tales, and a mother who walked away. She looked up and met Gerdie's gaze, wordless with incomprehension.

'Maybe you should then. It would ease both their minds.' But perhaps she saw something on Tinna's face at her words, because her own twisted and she added very gently, 'We would never send you away, Tinna. Lilith would never do that. This is your home.'

Somewhere in the house, Tinna's phone chimed and she would have put money just then on it being her mother, asking again about the hotel. It was not enough to be exiled as a child, now they wanted to take her away from it all once again. No, Tinna thought. Whatever their fears, she did not owe them this.

'I'll stay,' she said slowly. 'Nothing's going to happen to me.'

Gerdie nodded once. 'You'll stay away from the sea at night? Aside from ghosts, it's still not the safest place for someone with—' She waved a hand. '—physical difficulties. Is that how you say it?'

Tinna shrugged one shoulder and gave a nod, and if Gerdie misinterpreted what she was agreeing to, then that was not Tinna's fault. She had no intention at all of keeping away from the sea.

'Come then,' Gerdie said, her eyes sharp and not entirely fooled. 'Let's go swimming. Maybe it'll help you sleep.'

It didn't. Of course it didn't. It helped with the pain in her leg, and she thought for a moment when she first slipped beneath the steaming water that the fingers of her right hand tingled with half-felt heat. But perhaps not. Perhaps, like with so much, it was her mind playing a game of make-believe, constructing feeling from memory. If only, she thought later, lying on her bed staring out at the starlit dark, it worked the other way.

She had answered her mother's text with a Thank you, and a No. And her mother had not replied. She had talked to Lilith and Gerdie about education systems and tourism and Elías' family, and been just a little proud of herself for managing to do so without losing track of swathes of time. It had been almost nice, to talk about the world as if it were real and unbroken; it had also made Lilith relax her guard.

She was not waiting in the lounge tonight, and Gerdie had gone home. Either Tinna's performance earlier had been convincing or they had trusted her slantwise agreements to obey Lilith's rules. Tinna didn't much care which it was. When she was standing on the doorstep, leaning back against the closed door so that she could tilt her face to the sky, she cared only about this—the fact that she could breathe freely for the first time in two days. The air against her face was sharp as ice but the wind had died away entirely, the land lying like a great held breath and the sea just out of sight the only sound in the world.

She turned eventually and crossed the hagged grass of the garden, clambered slowly, cane-less, over the ridged bank above the beach and then down onto the black sand again. Pebbles click-clacked beneath her feet, the sea murmured a sibilant greeting in the shingle, and its surface stretching away to the drowned horizon was taut and still as the skin of a drum. Tinna went down the ink-black shore then lowered herself carefully to sitting above the waterline, slipping her boots off to ease the pinpricks and constriction, and wrapping her arms around her legs. She rested her chin on her knees and watched the somnolent movement of the water as it curled and receded two feet from her toes, curled and receded, whispering.

She thought of her grandmother coming down here when she and Elías had been children, all three of them asleep in the house and one woman crossing this black sand and walking into the water. No, she had been telling the truth to Lilith. There was no urge to throw herself beneath the waves, there was only the comfort in being alone and listened to and perhaps understood. The sea whispered, full of drowned snowflakes and melting glaciers and her family's ghosts. She sighed slowly, feeling herself unwind.

'The thing is,' she whispered back after a few minutes, 'that I don't see how I can move on until I can remember. I don't *want* to move on until I have remembered.' Or at all. The whole idea felt if not quite blasphemous, then surely impossible. An incoming wave touched her toes. 'The thing is,' she whispered slowly, unfurling a truth, 'I am so angry.'

The sea hummed a note that lifted the hairs on her arms. The stars swung infinitesimally across the sky. She had said it, and the world did not stop. The waves curled around her toes again, colder against the arch of her feet than even the stones. 'It is not fair,' she said to the endless miles of black water. 'It is not fair that not only do I lose *him*, but I must also lose my *memory of him*. It is not fair and that makes me so angry.'

Give her back to me.

She didn't care where this constructed voice was coming from. Perhaps it was even his, distorted by the sea and the fractures in her mind. She only cared that the sea listened and understood. Of course it understood—what was an ocean made of if not tears and bones?

'Yes. I'd do anything to have that back. To have that time with him back.'

To have *him* back but even now, even half-sedated and desperate, she knew what was impossible and what wasn't. She could not have him, but by god, she'd do anything to have her memories of him. Their last kiss, their last argument, the last night of his weight beside hers in bed, his body's warmth, his humming in the kitchen, his smile like a promise.

I'm outside, are you coming?

Had she greeted him with a kiss, or had she not? Had they smiled at one another in the lilac summer evening? Had they argued, was that why… The car, the wet road. Or had they both been distracted, her checking her phone, him tapping his fingers to the radio? She hoped they had been talking. How much more terrible it would be if she had wasted those last few minutes thinking of anything other than him.

The sea sucked at her heels, pebbles laughing softly as they moved. Someone sighed, someone hummed a lullaby.

Vini mínum vagga ég í ró
En úti biður andlit á glugga
My love let me lull you to sleep
Outside waits a face at the window

She lifted her right hand and held it out in front of her, studying the outline of it against the sea. All the many forms of absence.

I cannot sleep.

'No,' she whispered.

I would give anything to have her back.

'Yes,' she whispered.

The sea reached her ankles and the tops of her thighs, soaking through her pyjamas, and even through the drugs and the wishing, the cold made her hiss. She tightened her arms around her bent knees.

I cannot sleep. I cannot sleep for she is gone.

Tinna closed her eyes. The waves curled around her like they were cradling her, like they were stopping her from falling.

I only want what is mine.

'Yes,' she whispered. She only wanted what was hers, what was likely somewhere within her already, but would not show itself. 'I only want what is mine. I'd give anything.'

Yes.

And she only realised she was crying because her tears were hot against the cold of her scars. Yes, she thought, her throat too close to drowning to speak. Yes, anything at all. Just their last kiss, or their last exchanged look. If she could only have one thing then could it be that? Or the last time he had taken her hand in his, the fit of their fingers, the heat of his palm. Could not the world give her just one thing to tether her because she was not strong enough to withstand this? *Please*, she thought as the sea wrapped itself around her hips, *please help me*.

Yes.

She bent her head, forehead to knees, tears falling from her closed eyes into the water that curled and eddied around her. Salt to salt, she thought, and darkness to darkness, and she would give anything at all.

Blood and bone.

The sea hummed, tugged at her as if asking her to dance. She did not move.

Blood and bone.

If only it was that easy, she thought. If blood and broken bones were sufficient tithe then she had surely given payment enough for a hundred small memories, a thousand.

The sea sighed; the pebbles beside her murmured.

Click-clacked against one another. *Click-clack*.

And Tinna opened her eyes without moving.

Wait, she thought. A different kind of cold crackled along her spine.

Someone sighed. The pebbles shifted *click-clack*.

Blood and bone.

She lifted her head. The sky was bereft of stars now, clouds engulfing the entire world so the darkness here on the shore was dense as tar. Why was she thinking of blood? The waves reached for her hips and curled around her ankles; her hands gripping her biceps were stiff with cold. The voice was her own mind, it was the sea as a mirror and an echo, it was the comfort of the broken, so why was she thinking of blood? Where was the comfort in that?

We only want what is ours. You and I, we only want what we are owed.

Tinna's mind emptied of everything at all. Tears stung her cheeks as they froze.

So will you give payment?

The stones beside her *click-clacked* quietly once, then once again. Just as they had beneath her own boots when she had walked down the shore.

She stared out at the abyssal sea, the water returned to tug at her like hands. Turn your head, Tinna, she told herself. Stand up. But her body was too used to betraying her now, and the water too cold. She didn't move. The sea inhaled, tugged her again. The stones clicked softly. *Click-clack.*

We only want what is ours, the lullaby voice murmured beside her in the darkness. *Give payment in blood and bone. Then we shall both have back what was taken.*

Chapter Nine

'What—' she tried to say, although she had no idea what she was asking, or even who; but the voice cut her off.

Vini mínum vagga ég í ró… I cannot sleep. I cannot sleep. Vini mínum vagga ég í ró. I cannot sleep. I cannot—

'No,' Tinna whispered, and finally, finally moved. Her hands on the sand, pushing herself to standing, her leg buckling, lancing her entire right side with pain so she landed in the water on her knees as the waves rose to touch her face, her lips her eyes.

'No,' she repeated, to the sea or her own body. Or her treacherous mind. Pushing again and this time managing to stay upright, her hands wide for balance as the tide pulled at her calves.

The only sound in the world was her own ragged breathing and the breaking waves, and she turned away, wishing herself faster, praying her leg held her up, feeling her way blindly up the beach through the tarry dark. The waves snarling in her pyjamas, wrapping around her ankles like hands, and she could hear her own pulse now, her teeth chattering with cold.

Then, just at the point where she was free of the water, she faltered.

The stones murmured then fell silent and someone… someone was there.

The night-time pressed against her and *someone was there*. If she lifted her hand she would touch them.

'Lilith?'

The sea breathed, quieter than her own breaths. It was nothing, she told herself. Nothing but the unearthly darkness and her own addled mind. Too cold and too wounded, fabricating—

Jáaa. Lilith.

—Fabricating voices. She curled her hands into fists, or thought she did.

Já. Lilith. She has refused payment. She doesn't understand. She sleeps.

'Stop it,' Tinna whispered to herself. She willed herself to take another step, but couldn't. To reach out her left hand and brush the empty air, but couldn't. She wished she had not spoken all her wishes aloud and made them real. Her heart beat desperately.

You understand. You cannot sleep. You will give payment and we shall both have back what was taken.

Oh god, she thought. This was madness. It was drugs and hallucinations. 'Okay,' she said, trying to speak firmly, as if to a child. Perhaps that was who she was talking to, her own lost child who had run on these beaches and wept against her brother in an empty house. 'How do I pay? How do I get him back?' The memory of him at least. The knowledge… please,

please, that he had not suffered at the end.

The night waited. She waited. The voice did not speak and she might have smiled if she was not once more so close to weeping. 'See? There's no answer is there? There's no payment I can make for this. There's nothing I can do to make this right.' She lifted a hand and pressed it against her chest, felt the beat of her heart and knew by that which hand she had raised. 'It is not fair. But none of this is.'

Bring her down to the sea in the dark. Give payment.

She laughed. The noise was shockingly loud, making her heart judder against her palm. She sounded like a madwoman talking to the empty night, laughing like a crone, breaking into pieces. The sand in front of her hissed and fell silent. Warm air touched her cheek and she remembered the window suddenly. The condensation there and gone in the dark.

I promise. I promise.

Then the clouds shifted and stars appeared in between them like pathways across the heavens, and the warmth on her cheek was gone. A wave fell in on itself with a crash, and she jerked as if waking. Pain flickered in her leg, her hip, her spine as she turned a full circle on the black sand above the high tide line. Nothing. Just her and a sea riffling in a new wind, and the stars making the world tangible again. God, she thought, what was happening to her?

I promise, the voice had said. And it had sounded so certain, as if she only had to believe it to win everything back. Sleep and sedatives were swimming through her veins now the fear was fading and it took an inhuman effort to take one step up the beach, and then another. She was so tired of being lost; it was so tiring to search and never find. Lightning traced her nerves and it would be the easiest thing in the world to just sink down onto the black sand and close her eyes.

She did not remember getting back to the house. But here she was, sitting on her bed, her bare feet still dusted with sand and her skin burning in the warmth. She had lost her boots, she realised. Washed away by that strange tide that had climbed up her limbs and not willingly let her go. There would be questions from Lilith and Gerdie, and possibly anger or guilt or both together, but just now she was too weary to care. She remembered her mother laughing, whispering, *a nøkker will lure you to a watery grave* and Elías rolling his eyes with all the superiority of his years while Tinna wriggled with delighted horror. She reached for her phone and sent her mother a message, only afterwards realising that she would not see it till morning.

  - Why did you stop telling us fairy tales?
  The words stayed unread and she set the phone aside, emptiness yawing in her mind where that voice and its terrible promises had echoed. She stared at her hands, black specks of sand dotting her pale palms and the sea beyond the window was almost too quiet to hear, as if it were listening for her reply.

Dreams chased her. The car, headlights on a wet road, him humming softly. She turned her head to look at him and in the light of a car passing the other way, he turned to her like a mirror. Only there were shadows over his face, swirling blue-black shadows that meant she could not see his eyes or his smile, and she wanted to reach out to touch him but her hands would not obey.

Don't you remember me? He said, and *oh* but his voice. Oh his beautiful voice reverberating through her heart like the purr of a cat.

'I'm trying to,' she whispered, willing her hands to move. If only she could touch him, reach through those serpentine shadows and run her fingers along the familiar lines of his cheekbones, his jaw, the lashes of his eyes. If only she could touch him it would be okay.

Don't you want to remember me? He said.

'Yes. Oh god yes. Ben, I do. So much. I miss you so much. Ben, I miss you.' And they weren't in the car now, but in a hedge maze, towering green all around like a sea in a storm, ahead of her a single iron door and his hand in hers. Oh thank god, she thought, but it was her right hand so she could not feel him. She could not feel the warmth of him, or the callouses that she loved against her skin. This was, she thought, her own mind. This maze of shadows and entanglement. And he was behind this door as well as beside her. All those missing moments, all those lasts that she wanted more than anything else, they were here through this iron door, three steps away if only—

You need the key, he whispered, his breath against her cheek, and she wanted to lean back into him, feel his arms come around her the way they had done several thousand times, and how many of those times had she not stopped to marvel at the wonder of it?

'How do I find it?' She pressed her free hand against the door, the chill against her palm sharp and familiar, the metal slick with water. He lifted their joined fingers, pressed her knuckles to his shadow-hidden lips but she couldn't feel it, she couldn't feel it and would burn down the world to do so. 'Ben, how do I find it?'

Tinna…

She turned her head from the gate back to him; he was further away from her now and she had not even felt him release her hand. 'Ben,' she gasped but could not move. Of course she could not move, when did dreams ever let you follow your heart? 'Ben, where is the key?'

He was fading, the maze was shifting around him, the hedges folding inward like waves. No, she thought, trying to wrench herself into motion, but everything was dense as blood around her, dense as tar.

Love, he whispered. *My love, we are made of tears and bone.*

She woke.

'Tinna,' her aunt called, as if she had called already.

Tinna blinked at the light beyond the window, three ravens crossing the high, battered blue of the sky. Her eyes were crusted with dried tears and when she moved, pain crashed through her like an angry beast. She froze, breathing slowly so that she did not cry out. Yes, she thought, it was true. She was made of tears and bone.

'Tinna, are you okay?'

'Yes,' she whispered, then louder, 'Yes, what—'

'Can I come in?

Tinna lifted a hand gingerly to her face, scrubbed her eyes clear. The ravens were still there, tangling their claws together to fall windmilling through the open air, then rising again, calling. Such faith, she thought, to bind yourself to another and fall. Such love. 'Okay,' she said, and began again, cautiously, to move.

Lilith watched her from the doorway, and the cat passed her with his tail high, leapt up onto the bed just as Tinna got herself to sitting. He walked back and forth across her legs twice then settled into a semi-circle by her knee. A bass clef cat, a clouded curlicue. Tinna reached for the tablets and the glass on the table beside her, focusing carefully on waveforms and the ravens tumbling, and not on the long minutes that stood between taking these medicines and the abatement of the pain.

She set the glass down and as if this was what Lilith had been waiting for, she shifted and spoke.

'I heard you, that was why I knocked. I thought—'

Tinna reached out and brushed the cat's spindrift fur. He began to purr. 'Just a dream,' she said. 'Sorry if I woke you.'

'No, I was up.' Lilith said. 'Do you want tea? Or coffee? I was thinking we might go up the coast today. A short walk at Ytri-Tunga. It's a golden beach and there are usually seals there. Would you…' her voice trailed off, looking at the floor in front of her. Tinna followed her gaze.

There was sand on the pale wood of the floor. Black sand in the shape of her bare feet.

Lilith stared at them a moment longer and then met Tinna's eyes, looking unbearably wary and hurt.

'I lost my boots,' Tinna heard herself say. As if that were the explanation that Lilith wanted. As if it was the bare feet and not the sand.

Lilith's eyes narrowed, a frown forming on her forehead. 'No, you didn't,' she said, and jerked her head towards the window. 'They're there.'

And they were. Tucked neatly beneath the window, the floorboards under them dark with water and the only thing Tinna could think to say was, 'Oh. Your floor.'

But she remembered sitting here on this bed in the dark,

studying her bare feet and imagining her boots drifting on the tide, sinking with barely a ripple. She had left them behind, they would have been swallowed by the tide. That was real, wasn't it? She was not so far gone that she'd misremembered that.

She studied the wet boots again, the canvas dark and a thin trail of seaweed clinging to the heel, a flower-stem tangled in the laces, blue buds crushed and wet… What if… What if it hadn't been her shattered mind conjuring voices…

Will you give payment?

She shuddered; the pain moved through her like shoaling fish. And he was there again, in her mind like he had been in her dream, his face hidden but his voice like her own heart cracked open.

Don't you want to remember me?

Yes, she thought, just like in her dream. Oh god yes.

Her phone buzzed peremptorily and Tinna jerked her gaze away from the sea-soaked, sea-returned boots. Lilith stepped further into the room and reached for the phone, then handed it to her without speaking. Tinna glanced at the screen, saw Elías' name and set the phone down again. Their mother had told them fairy stories, and then she had stopped. Their mother wanted her to go to Reykjavík, and their aunt was looking at Tinna as if the sand on the floor were a far worse thing than the scars on her face, the ring on her finger, the pain. Perhaps the whole world was more broken than it appeared. Köttur purred and her thoughts were slippery and inchoate. *Where is the key? We are made of tears and bone.* What if it was real? At least a little bit.

We will both have back what was taken.

What if she could?

Impossible.

But she was a construct of impossibilities now.

Lilith moved again and Tinna blinked, not knowing how long she had been staring at nothing and thinking fantastical things. Terrible things.

Incomprehensible things, and yet what was more incomprehensible than grief? What was more fantastical than living? What was more terrible than forgetting? What wouldn't she give?

Nothing at all.

'Was there anyone there? Why didn't you wake me, I would have…' She trailed off.

'Stopped me,' Tinna whispered. She felt weirdly calm.

'Did you meet anyone? Was anyone there?'

Yes. 'No.'

Lilith nodded once, her hand twitched as if about to reach for the cat, but other than that she was holding herself very still. Tinna recognised it, the bracing against the world, and might have felt guilty if she weren't hurting so much.

'So. Ytri-Tunga? And then we could go to Gerdie's. We could stay at Gerdie's.'

Tinna lifted her gaze to her aunt's then and almost smiled. 'Sending me away, Lilith?' she asked softly. 'I won't come to any harm from the sea, how many times must I tell you? There is nothing it can take from me that I haven't already lost.'

'There is always more to lose,' her aunt said with an edge, a familiar snap that was so much easier to navigate than her fear.

Pain dragged its claws down Tinna's leg and she rubbed at it with her numb hand pointlessly, impatience beginning to snarl at the back of her mind, and her voice only level because the pain demanded it. 'I am not my grandmother,' she said, glancing back out once at the sky, devoid of birds. 'I am not trying to drown, I am only trying to find a little peace, a little healing.' A key to the locked door in her own mind. 'The sea offers me that.'

She listened to her own words. And to those other words in the darkness, and wanted nothing more than to be alone so that she could *think*. What wouldn't she try? Anything. *You will give payment and we shall both have back what was taken.* Did she even care if it were real or not when it might unlock her own mind?

'Ytri-Tunga then, and tonight we'll walk with you.'

Tinna shifted, tensing against the pain, tried to focus on Lilith and what Lilith was saying. 'Umm, no thank you,' she said after a long moment. 'I don't... I'd better just stay here today. Sorry.'

Lilith looked from her to the boots to the window and back again. The frown had not left her eyes and her hair was tangled as if she had been running her hands through it ceaselessly. 'You're sure?'

Tinna tried to move her leg and discovered that the painkillers had not reached her nerves yet. She sank back gingerly, hissing out a breath.

'I'm sure,' she whispered. The room smelled of iodine and deep water.

'Bad today is it?' Lilith's face was tight and pale and Tinna could see where her fingers were digging into her waist. She wondered what Lilith was holding in, with that grip. What was being silenced. 'Is that because you got cold last night?'

There might have been a barb in the question. If it were her sister, there would have been. Tinna didn't particularly care. 'It doesn't need a reason,' she said simply. 'It's just bad some days.' The cat pressed his paws into her knee, his claws catching on the duvet and his purr like a distant engine. Tinna thought of the fisherman in his black boat and the man on the shore, and wondered if there was anyone she could ask any of the questions in her mind.

Lilith stepped backward, one hand coming up to grip the doorframe. 'You stay there then. I'll bring you coffee and toast before I go, and your cane.'

So like her sister. The barbs and the shutters, the constrained kindness; and if Tinna had always read it as near-lovelessness, perhaps that was excusable. A child does not believe her parent capable of fear.

But what if it *was* real?

'Where is it?' she said just as Lilith was stepping away. 'Where's the grave?'

Lilith turned back.

'Your grandmother's? It's—'

'The child's. The daughter's.'

Lilith stared. The sea whispered and a stonechat called from the garden like pebbles tapping together. *Click-clack.* Somewhere the sun came out, brightening the water, but not the light here in this room.

'You believe me? About what happened? If you believe me, why do you risk it?'

Tinna looked away, trying to tether the edges of the

night's strange happenings to herself now this morning, contemplating the unbelievable.

'My mother used to tell us fairy stories,' she said slowly. Her fingers moved on her thighs and the cat cracked open one eye. 'I'd forgotten.'

She didn't look back to her aunt, instead pressing each fingertip of her right hand down in turn, watching them, trying to tell herself that things which were lost were not gone.

'Where's the child's grave, Lilith?' she repeated.

Chapter Ten

But Lilith said she didn't know. And she said Tinna ought not be leaving the house if she was so sore, and then she left Tinna to her breakfast and promised, steely-eyed, to be back again by five. An hour passed, or perhaps less, or more, before Tinna remembered her phone.

- Have you spoken to mum today? She's not answering her phone?

Of course she wasn't, Tinna thought. The blue ticks against her late night message ought to have told her to expect that.

- I asked questions. She'll speak to you tmrw.

- Ah. What kind of questions?

Tinna stared at her phone, trying to summon the will and the words. She wanted to rest her head back against the pillow and stare out into the deceptive blue of the sky, weighing pain and disbelief and desperation as she waited for the ravens to return.

- About her and Lilith?

She sighed, touched her left hand to the long, fiery line of her thigh, then answered.

- About fairy tales. About ghosts and grandmother's death and what she was frightened of when we left.

-…okay then no wonder she's not speaking to us! Why ghosts?

And Tinna understood what Lilith had meant now, that it was easier not to explain. A few months ago she would have laughed at herself. A few months ago she would never have stood in a mapless dark being whispered to by the sea, or she might, but she wouldn't have been listening. Her boots were slowly drying beneath the window, shedding sand like a skin.

- So there's a family story of a ghost who haunts us. Lilith says he drowned grandmother, and her sister.

She remembered the fisherman on the shore and wondered if he would have known more, and whether he would be out there today on his boat or on the beach. If she met him again, perhaps she would ask him for his version of the tale.

- wow really? That's crazy.

Was it? Köttur stirred, twitched one ear, and began to purr again.

- Wait. You're saying we left because of a ghost story?? Seriously?

- Maybe

- omfg

She didn't reply. How could she say, *yes, but if you'd stood beside me in the dark you might be half-believing too*, when it wasn't true. You had to be broken first, she thought, before you would be willing to listen to the promises the sea offered.

We are made of tears and bone. No, he'd not understand that.

A moment later,

- That's the most ridiculous thing ever. I can't imagine mum believing anything like that. If Lilith did, maybe that's what they fought about.

It was what Tinna had thought, but she remembered whispering in a woodland, the willows mink-green all around them. She remembered her mother urging her to go to a hotel.

- She used to tell us fairy stories & she stopped. I think she believes too.

He didn't answer for a while, the painkillers began to erode at the very edges of the pain and she held herself still, waiting it out, her gaze drifting between her boots and the hanging silver sky. Thinking of the thick black darkness on the beach when she had ceased to be alone.

- Well now I'm mad instead of amused.

Yes, thought Tinna. She had thought that too—the waste of it. But now it felt inevitable. If they had not left then she would not have met Ben, if he had not died she would not have returned to listen to the sea speaking her own longings into the dark. Perhaps the sea and all its ghosts had set its claws in her years ago, when she had run along its borders with her brother, and since then she had always been on her way home.

Her phone pulsed again, she sighed and looked at it.

- She tore us away from our home because of a ghost story. She shut us out because of a ghost story. I can't believe it.

- she thought she was protecting us

- That doesn't make it ok.

Didn't it? She honestly couldn't tell. And she had no energy to spare for Elías' anger so she did not attempt a reply.

It took until after lunch before she could gather all her frayed edges together enough to leave the house. Whether it was the cold, like Lilith had said, or the dream or just the terrible rawness of having spoken her wishes and her anger aloud, the pain was fiercer today than it had been for weeks. Even with the drugs it was jag-toothed, clawed and spined, and quartering her bones like a beast searching for prey and every time she moved, or every time she didn't move, it hurt more.

She thought—if thought was the word, more a formless wanting—of the hot pools Gerdie had taken her to. But Gerdie was not here, and the monster was.

Then in the afternoon, two doses away from the damage of the night, the beast slowed its pacing of the confines of her bones, and she breathed deeper. Smelling the seaweed tangled in her boots, sulphur from the shower, the fading notes of coffee from the morning. And coming to a decision, aware even as she did so of what was at stake and how much of that was her own sanity.

That's crazy, Elías had said. But she would do anything to find her memories of him. She would believe anything, and perhaps it made a terrible sort of sense that her broken mind might set itself fabricated challenges built around a myth as it followed breadcrumbs through the dark.

Certain actions, places, smells, might trigger memory recall, the psychiatrist had said. *You might find that the most unexpected thing can prompt your subconscious and unlock a door, so to speak.*

Unlock a door, she thought, rubbing her right hand over the suture marks on her cheek. She didn't need it to be real, she only needed it to be a key.

The church waited in the pale blue light, blacker than the cliffs behind it but rendered fragile by the miles of snow and the mountains. One car in the car park and the existence of other people momentarily startled her, as if this headland was a kingdom just for her, and her ghosts and her redemption. She reached the lych gate and paused there for a moment to take the weight from her leg, ease the fingers of her left hand where they had been gripping the cane. There were three tourists over the other side, taking photos in their poppy-red barely-worn waterproof coats, the vowels of their distant voices round with satisfied wonder. One of them glanced at her, glanced again, then looked carefully away, and Tinna pushed on unevenly into the graveyard. The green grass rising through the night's snow, and the grey stones, the black wood and white paint swam around her like painted eels and her own limbs were floating. The only thing tethering her was the pain, the thought of keys and blood and mourning, and the presence of the tourists like an audience.

It would be an old grave, but most of them here were old, and half of them were barely legible, so the task felt hopeless even before she'd begun, but she did it anyway. Moving slowly, running the fingers of her free hand over old dates like braille.

'Where are you?' she whispered. There were yellow stars of cinquefoil like eyes against the snow in the lee of the graves and the dark furtive shadow of a wren moving through the stones of the wall, and Tinna watched all of it, waiting for another breadcrumb with a brittleness that was as much the opiates as it was the desperation.

'Excuse me,' a voice said, and Tinna looked up, her cane catching in the grass as she turned, but the tourist had not been talking to her, they were talking to another man she had not noticed before. He was standing a few metres away, closer to the wall, his back to Tinna so that all she could see was the tourist's keen smile and her two companions standing by the church wall, waiting.

'Excuse me, would you mind taking our picture?' she said,

east coast American, one arm stretching forward, and Tinna could not see but guessed she was holding out her phone. The newcomer's head tilted, his dark hair restless in the wind and he made no other move at all; he did not answer and Tinna inhaled sharply. Oh, she thought. Here it was.

'I'm sorry, I don't speak…' The woman had not dropped her arm but her smile had tightened and colour that was not from the wind was rising beneath her light brown cheeks. 'Do you speak English?' she said slowly. 'O Español?'

Tinna took a step forward; the woman shot her a glance over the man's shoulder and the look in her eyes was so conflicted that Tinna almost laughed. The silent man or the woman made of scars, which was more unnerving? But they would never find out, because he turned toward Tinna and, as if the American did not exist at all, said softly, in Icelandic, 'You were looking for her. She's here.' And gestured with one heavy hand to the grave at his feet.

Tinna took the three steps to reach him, and stared down at the headstone with the world bursting into fractals around her, a woman's voice whispering 'I'm sorry, I didn't realise. I'll leave you alone.' The wren alarm calling high and piercing as a blade and her own blood beating in her ears like the sea.

'The girl?' she said, as if this conversation made any sense at all.

But the man nodded, the light angleward across his face leaving his eyes in shadow.

Someone had laid flowers recently on the girl's grave, the headstone had a white streak of lichen like a scar and canted seaward as if yearning for the water. Familiarity swam through her as she rested a hand on the stone. *Hello*, she thought. *Hello again*. The flowers were the same as the ones on the windowsill that Lilith had thrown away, and the stem tangled in her boot laces this morning, and Tinna remembered them now. These glass-blue bells were the smjörgras that grew all along the shore. She stared at them, her mind full of the feel of their stems clutched in her own childish hand, and then full of roses yellow as a sunrise and then lilies white as bone. Who had left them here, she wondered, was it Lilith? And why? As if anything—hurt or heartbreak or broken bones—could be healed by something that was already dying.

'How did you know I was looking?' she said, feeling her own distance from her mother tongue like an exiling. 'Do you know the story? About her father?'

She watched the man and when he only studied the flowers, added belatedly, 'I'm Tinna. Are you Árni Leifsson?' It felt like they had moved past niceties long ago, like they hadn't only spoken once before, briefly, as strangers.

The tourists walked past them slowly, all three throwing sidelong glances their way, the fabric of their coats rustling and the wren calling again once before falling silent. Car doors slammed, the engine bursting into life then dying away until the only sounds left were the wind carving pathways across the fields, the distant fulmars and the nearer sea; and the man lifted his gaze from the grave to her.

There was grey in his beard and grey in his eyes that might have been iris, or age, or reflected snow. She could not imagine this man being friends with Gerdie.

He dipped his head like a crow, and Tinna breathed out sharply, oddly relieved. 'You are Jóhanna's daughter, yes? Come home.'

His Icelandic was oddly lilting and the sea murmured as he spoke, making the space between them seem vaster than just the reach of an arm. But he was just a neighbour, an old fisherman with idiotic chickens back from the north early. Of course he was; what else could he possibly be? 'Yes, I am. Did Gerdie tell you?' And what had Gerdie told him, and what other secrets did he know?

He lifted one weather-cracked hand, pale as linen to rest it on the gravestone. Not leaning, she thought, but like you might touch the head of an old and weary hound, gently, full of kindness. Somewhere here alongside this girl must lie his own kin, a long ancestry of hardship and strength and the sea. He made a low humming sound of agreement and the sea answered, the wind curled around them sharply. There were so many things Tinna wished she knew but right now there was only one. The next step of her breadcrumb trail. In the briar-tangle of her pain it was the only thing she could focus on.

'Did you know my mother, before she left?' If he knew this, then he might know why.

He laughed. Or she thought he did, although beneath the beard and with his eyes shadowy, the smile that ought to have come with it was impossible to see.

'Oh, yes. There is no peace in leaving. She has learned this yet?'

Tinna shook her head very slightly, Her hair wove webs across her face and she lifted a hand to brush it away, her fingers like ice against her eyelids. He understood, she thought. 'You know why…' But she hesitated there. It seemed cruel to mention her death standing over her grave. It had seemed crueller still to talk about his life, at the funeral, to talk about his laughter and his warmth like they were not hatchets carving at her bones. But she had scarcely been listening anyway, whereas now beneath the ragged shroud of the sky, she was. And anyway nothing about this felt normal, so perhaps this was the

only time she *could* ask about drownings and vengeance, here
at a child's grave with a stranger. Beneath Lilith's thick coat, her
skin was alive with cold and unease, but still… she had been
looking for a key… 'Do you remember my grandmother?'

This time she saw his smile, white and snaggle-toothed
within his beard. 'I do. I do. Do you remember?'

'No,' she said. And then helplessly, 'I want to.'

A gull called long and unanswered.

'Are you sure?' he said in his canting voice, bending his
head to study the grave again; the light shifted greyer and the
shadows deepened. 'I see her in you still. I remember you as a
girl along the shore. Always running, never alone.'

He said this like it was connected to his question, and
Tinna understood. 'But I'm alone now,' she whispered. 'And
I'm certainly not running.'

'Yes, that is it. The mother ran, but the daughter came
home.' She thought he smiled again, although it was hard to
tell, and then he curled the hand on the headstone into a fist
and withdrew it. Took a step back, his feet silent in the thin
snow. 'That is fitting, Jóhanna's daughter. Perhaps you will
find what you are looking for then.' He took another step, half
turned, then looked back at her to add, 'Give my greetings to
Lilith. Bring her to meet me, tell her it's been too long.'

Tinna turned her head reflexively towards the house and by
the time she looked back, Árni Leifsson was walking beneath
the lych gate, made phantasmagorical by a wind whipping up
the snow into figurines that danced and died, danced and died
silently.

He hadn't told her what he knew of the ghost and the girl, and
Tinna might have been more frustrated by that if she wasn't
here, where she had wanted to be. The next breadcrumb.

Let an old fisherman keep his secrets and his gossip. Perhaps it was good that he was not inclined to share, he certainly seemed to judge her mother for leaving so perhaps she was, to him, simply another tourist come seeking false connections. The wren slipped mouselike back along the wall, and Tinna pressed her left hand to her face, the ridges and punctuation of her scars beneath her palm like a code. She breathed in the salt-ice air, waited out a wave of clawing pain and forgot about Árni Leifsson entirely.

'So now what?' she whispered to herself, and perhaps also to the girl who had died and birthed a story.

Blood and bone, the voice had said. The voice come from her own hopes and Lilith's fisherman follower vengeful spirit dragging in from the sea for his tithe. And Tinna didn't mind shedding a little more for him, here, to add to the oceans she had shed for nothing other than her own life.

She dropped her cane then lowered herself carefully to kneeling, the snow soaking through her jeans and as she breathed through the pain, her lungs filled with the scent of winter, high places and old lavaflows. Such a scarred land, she thought again, as her leg subsided once more into its grinding ache. The wren began to sing and she wished she knew the girl's name and what had happened and how she had died. It seemed important now, to know this child's last days that had led to the destruction of a family one hundred years later.

Leaning forward tentatively, she ran her left hand over the lichen-drowned words, but failed to make sense of them, so reached instead into her pocket. And pulled out a knife.

Chapter Eleven

She had thought it would be better to cut her right hand, safer than trusting senseless fingers with a blade, but she stared at the welling blood, at the dividing line of skin and flesh, and was frightened for the first time since that moment last night in the unleavened darkness when she had felt breath on her cheek and been unable to move. It was so *wrong* to bleed and not feel it. Which was why she needed to do this. Know the exact parameters of her loss so that she could grieve it fully. She tilted her hand and watched blood trail a heavy line across her skin. Salt and hurt and broken hearts, she thought, the bird still singing like a voice from another world. Here, she thought. Let this be the key. Let this be the trail that will lead me to him.

The blood shone on the snow, catching the light redly like eyes at night. Slipping in between ice crystals as it carved a path to the buried earth and for a moment she saw something. A flicker-flash of red lights and red blood black in the blackness, rain on broken glass, someone calling her name.

Yes, she thought, closing her eyes, curling her bleeding hand into a fist. Yes, please.

Red lights, rain on broken glass. Please, she thought.

Remember.

But it was gone.

It was gone. The wren had stopped singing. She unfurled her numb hand and studied the Rorschach painting of her blood on her palm. Red lights and red blood and someone calling. She strained for it, leaning forward over that wound she could not feel, urging her whole body towards that moment of *something*. Please, anything.

But there was nothing there. It had not, she realised, even been him calling. A paramedic perhaps, or a fireman, but if not him then it hardly mattered. She closed her eyes again, breathing slowly so that she did not shout, or howl or weep. All of them would make the pain worse, and none of them would solve anything at all.

She sat there for a long time, the storms in her nerves slowly escalating, and her tattered mind spinning on itself. If this was not enough, if this was not the right series of acts to trigger remembering, not the right trail of breadcrumbs, then… then was it all a lie, or was it just that she, in the light of day, had strayed from the path?

Behind her closed eyes, the sea swirled red and shadowy, and she touched her left hand to her right, remembering his hand doing the same in her dream, remembering her heart breaking all over again because she could not feel him.

'Ben,' she whispered.

It was not often she said his name aloud, or even thought it. Because 'Ben' was the word she had whispered against his neck and shouted across a railway station and said a dozen times a day without noticing. It was carved so deep into her heart that to say it was like bleeding. But she said it now, and bled, and waited whilst despair eddied within her, circling the absences, the locked door, the memory of a stranger's voice whispering, *Bring her down to the sea in the dark. Give payment.*

Bring her down to the sea in the dark.

It wasn't true. She thought. How could that be an unlocking of her own mind.

I promise, he had whispered against her skin. *I promise.*

It couldn't be true.

Only… Lilith thought it was. And Tinna's own mother maybe thought it was. Árni Leifsson had said there was no peace in leaving, like he had known about ghosts and hauntings, and even Gerdie had said, *it seems wiser not to assume they're not real.*

Which made it all into something other than the entirely fantastical, didn't it? Something that might even be solid enough to carry hope.

But. But just because something might be not entirely untrue did not mean it was wise, or safe. Where was the wisdom or the safety in going down to the sea in the dark to give payment?

Something screamed above her and she flinched; the pain flared and spiked, the world swam and when she opened her eyes all she could see were the stars. But then her vision cleared and when the scream came again she looked up. It was an eagle, vast and far away, fulmars circling around it and parting before it like iron filings. They cried and wheeled and the eagle drifted a wide arc along the parabola of the mountainsides like the centre of a storm, then flexed its wings once, flipped sideways once, and high over Tinna's head a fulmar's white wings batted death throes in its claws. The eagle flew on inexorable and the other fulmars' cries lost their sharpness as they returned to their cliffs. The snow drifted in the rising breeze and the church creaked once, like a judgement.

Such a small death, she thought. So unimportant; apart from to the bird who died, the chick on the ledge, the eagle.

Did she even want wisdom, or safety, if weighed against remembering? She was the abandoned bird, the dying one, the endlessly hungry one. There was nothing she would not do.

Slowly, her left hand on her cane and her right on the blood-fed, bone-fed earth, she pushed herself to standing. The sun was drifting slipshod through ragged clouds and the land and sea were a motile patchwork of light and dark. She did not really understand what the voice in the dark was asking for but she understood *why*.

You understand. You cannot sleep. You will give payment and we shall both have back what was taken.

Tonight then, she thought. If not beneath sunlight and at the child's feet then beneath the moon and at the sea's. She should have guessed. Everything do to with love and locked doors happens beneath the moon.

*

Half an hour after Tinna returned, shivering and bloodstained, to the house, Lilith came home too, precisely at five as promised. Tinna washed her numb hand, remembering the doctor's cautions, took another dose of painkillers and Lilith said she was going out again, supermarket shopping down the coast. Did Tinna want to come, if only to sit in the car? No, Tinna thought, she did not want to leave this strip of land between graveyard and the sea. She was bound to it now by the cut on her palm and the death of the fulmar. By a dead man's promises and a dead man's absences. Had Tinna seen the aurora forecast, it looked good for later if it stayed clear? No, Tinna had not. She closed her eyes, green tendrils crossing her mind like flames. She did not know, when Lilith's car rumbled down the track and away, whether she had actually spoken any of her answers aloud. All of her body fusing itself molten and brittle and blazing around a mind bent on tonight and what she might do, down there on the shore, to forge herself a key.

And then Lilith returned in the draggling day, and Tinna woke, or at least resurfaced from the sea, to her aunt looking down at her warily, sadly.

'Bad still?' she said when Tinna shifted, winced, stilled again.

'Mmm.'

'Anything I can do?'

She doesn't understand. She sleeps.

'No. Thank you.' Tinna tried to move again, realised slowly that some of the inertia in her limbs was the cat on her lap, and that her right hand was pressed gently into his fur. Perhaps, sleeping, her numb hand had dreamed of comfort.

Time slipped. Lilith was setting a mug of tea down beside her. Lowering herself into the chair opposite. Köttur rose, stretched upwards making a silver sickle moon of his body, then resettled the other way.

'Equinox tonight,' Lilith said.

'Mmm.' Conversation felt beyond her. As if she had finally drifted a little too far from shore to tether herself at all.

'You must stay in, Tinna. I don't care if you believe me or not, but please promise this. I just need to know you are safe.'

I promise.

'Have you ever asked?' she heard herself say.

Lilith leaned back. The sea beyond the window carved curlicues of hidden currents, blue and grey. 'For him to stop?'

Tinna moved her head very slightly. Fires crackled in her spine. 'For forgiveness,' she said.

'I've done nothing wrong, I shouldn't have to.'

It startled Tinna a bit, her aunt's umbrage. She wanted to laugh. To say, it doesn't matter. When the universe destroys you, the universe owes you, if nothing else, its sorrow. *It is fitting*, Gerdie's friend had said. He was right.

'People always say sorry,' she whispered. 'Sorry for your loss. I'm so sorry that happened to you.'

'But that's not—'

'We are all culpable for each other's broken hearts.' She breathed in, lightning flickered in her leg, she breathed out again. 'We are all made of tears and bones,' she said. 'Like the sea.'

'Tinna—'

And now the words had begun they didn't wish to stop, not speaking to Lilith so much as speaking to make something true. 'I am not frightened of pain, or blood or penance. I am not frightened of ghosts, or of the dark, only of being alone in it. Living forever with my hand pressed against a closed door, wishing for what was lost.'

'So don't live like that.' Lilith's voice cut through the stormwaters welling around her. Hard and harsh and so like

Tinna's mother that their faces blurred in front of her. Their voices blending until it was both of them speaking, and both of them failing to understand. 'Move on, Tinna. It does no good to hang onto things you cannot change. Look what happened to the fylgjendur. Look at what comes of a refusal to grieve and heal and move on. Look how much you can destroy.'

'It's not…' But the storm had subsided, or moved from her voice to her bones, and she fell silent, pushing Köttur gently from her lap to clamber gracelessly to her feet. Remembering even then to keep her right hand curled, hiding the cut within. The sun was grazing the skin of the mountaintops, the sky sinking through shades of blue as the evening star woke over the sea. Soon, Tinna thought. Soon. And it was not a refusal to grieve what she had lost. It was a wanting to be able to treasure what little she had left.

Lilith opened her mouth to speak then closed it again.

'I want to remember,' Tinna said softly. 'I just want to remember.' She could taste iron on her tongue, she could taste salt and anger. 'Goodnight, Lilith,' she said, and turned away.

'Wait.' Lilith rose to her feet too, and when Tinna turned unsteadily, she reached out a hand slowly, carefully touching Tinna's cheek. 'Oh elskan mín,' she said, like she had once before. 'Forgive the world what it has done to you. Perhaps then you will remember. Be patient.'

Tinna looked from her aunt's too-familiar gaze to the long reach of the sea. She thought of the chick on the cliffs, hungry and helpless; and the eagle, hungry and hunting. She looked back to her aunt. 'I can't,' she said.

Elías had messaged her three times. She sat on the bed and read them once, then twice, then set her phone down and stared at the merciless skyline for a long time before replying. The first message was forwarded from their mother, the other two from him.

- *I'm going away for a few days. Enjoy your holiday and we'll talk when you return. Mum x*

- *Why am I even surprised. I'm going to come to you once we're back, ok? Don't blame yourself for mum running off again. This is on her and I'm so fucking sick of it, T. I really am.*

And then, twenty minutes after those two:

- *Let me know if she calls you?*

Tinna typed slowly, thinking that for once it was perhaps not a terrible thing to be unable to feel herself forming the words.

- *I will. It's okay. I love you.*

She pushed her phone and twenty-year old memories away, and realised she had not passed on the message from Árni Leifsson, but it could wait till morning. Everything from her fled mother to her aunt's fears could wait until morning, after Tinna had gone down to the sea and then come home again, carrying her broken heart within her like a chalice.

She took her tablets and waited for the sun to drop behind the mountains, then waited more for it to drop beneath the world. She did not mean to sleep but did anyway, water all around her like she was on the kayak again, rocking slowly. She heard voices, first Árni Leifsson saying, *I remember you as a girl running along the shore*, then the sea's voice asking for blood, and then finally Ben; and Ben, and Ben. Blue lights flashing, and red ones, and red blood shining blackly. Then just the wet road reflecting headlights and she turned her head and for a moment—her heart leapt—for a moment he looked back at her and smiled. Oh, she thought, Oh there you are, lifting a hand to touch his cheek... and waking.

And the memory already retreating back into a mist as impenetrable as an iron door, but she did not bother chasing it this time. Because the room was full of darkness and the sea was waiting. She was so close now she could almost feel the clasp of his fingers around her right hand. And it was as if that was why it had been numb since her waking, because it would only become alive again for this, for him. Surely this time she would remember. Her hand was pressed against the door and the key was made of tears and bone, so she would find it in the sea. Now, beneath the moon. She must.

*

The house was quiet, dark, catless, and it only took a few minutes to find boots and coat and be out the door, reaching the beach almost febrile with hope. Surely this time. Ben, she thought. His face turning to her in the car, it was there at the edge of her mind like a promise. The tide was coming in, opalescent waves breaking over the black sand and that stark contrast was so familiar it startled her all over again. How the parsimonious beauty of the beach set up an ache within her, the lonely house that her mother had grown up in, and her mother's mother, and back to before the village in the bay was abandoned. To when the child had died. She suspected she would always have ended up here, even if she had not been broken. Always coming home, just like a stranger in a graveyard had said.

She slipped her boots off as she had before and moved down to the waves, the cold shocking, the myriad blacks of the sand whispering around her feet.

Vini mínum vagga ég í ró
En úti biður andlit á glugga

The sea breathed. Her skin where it touched her sang and stung with cold. She closed her eyes and listened to the voices that her broken mind was giving the sea, that had driven her mother away and her aunt into silence. The drugs were oceanic within her, letting her sway effortlessly between hope and a terrible, sweeping melancholy that did not feel entirely her own.

A wave wrapped around her knees and she staggered, tipped forward then stepped back instinctively but unstartled. She had been waiting, she realised, fuddled by drugs and lullabies, for the tide to find her again.

People from this house go down to the sea at night, and drown, Lilith had said. Tinna stepped back again. She had replied that she was not suicidal, but she was only half-present and the waves were hungry; perhaps that was what had happened with her grandmother. Two young grandchildren in the house, exhaustion and forgetfulness. And then Lilith had constructed myth around bereavement, and lost what remained of her kin. *We are all culpable for each other's broken hearts*, Tinna had told her. She ought to have been kinder. But kindness would have meant promising to stay in bed, and she could not give her that.

She retreated up above the tideline, out of reach of the hungry waves and sat on a rock watching the sea rise and the stars blink awake in the deepening sky. She had thought, and planned and tried blood. Which had failed. So she did not think now, or try to map a pathway. She was in a maze of her own making and the sea, too, defied cartography so she would wait, and watch, and see where the salt in her blood and the tears in the ocean led her. The tide rose and even though she was cold she didn't move as the water gathered shadows and starlight. If she were lucky the aurora might appear. She tipped her head to the sky and waited, humming lullabies that sometimes were answered and sometimes were not.

It was the equinox, so Lilith believed he would come.

It was Ben's face turning towards hers, and an iron door waiting, so Tinna believed he would come.

The aurora came first. And as it spiralled across the stars Tinna realised two things she ought to have noticed before. That a light had come on in the house behind her, and the tide was up amongst the boulders here at the top of the beach. She looked at it lying calm and heavy around her, reflecting silver and shimmering greens faintly, soughing just inches from Tinna's feet high above where the strandline had been.

Vini mínum vagga ég í ró, the sea murmured beside her, and she wanted so badly, so very badly and without warning, to step down off her rock into the perfect black swell. *My love let me lull you to sleep.* It would be so peaceful, and she owed them this much.

She owed…

Tinna frowned, lifted her left hand to touch first her right, then the scars on her face, the regrowing hairline. No, that was not the promise. The promise was… it was that she would make payment, that they would both remember, and sleep.

'I came down to the sea in the dark,' she whispered. 'If I make payment will I have him back?'

The sea held a thousand stars, or perhaps it was all those swallowed snowflakes still there, whole and shining. She wanted to look up at the aurora, to lose herself in wonder, but could not tear herself from the drowning stars, the black swell, the singing.

You understand. You cannot sleep.

'Yes.' She trailed her right hand in the water, marvelling at the ink-black-silver of it. She didn't want to think. She just wanted to follow the trail left by her heart and the sea, and if she followed it through the darkness then perhaps… perhaps… their last shared smile, their last words, the last time he had held her hand in his, the last time he had said her name.

Ben, she thought. Ben, I'll find you.

It was not so much to ask. It was everything and nothing and the aurora unfurled above her, ribbons of green and vermilion painting waves and wounds across the sky and Tinna watched it now with her heart wide open, bleeding beauty and longing like a mirror. Pain seared her nerves and the lullaby rose, compelling.

We shall both have back what was taken.

It would be peaceful at least, she thought again, or someone else thought, and they were owed their blood. She sat on the rock, surrounded by the sea which was made of tears and bones. The water splashed gently once, then twice, then a third time.

You came home.

Oh, she thought.

You want to remember.

Oh.

It is fitting.

She turned to the man beside her and found herself smiling. 'It's you.'

Chapter Twelve

The man tipped his head slightly, the light of the sky unearthly in his eyes, catching on dark hair and greying beard. The sea curled around him like a great black cat. She should have known.

Perhaps part of her had, because she felt nothing so much as recognition now. Certainly no fear, not of this man who understood.

'I have waited so long,' he said. 'I have laid a thousand flowers on her grave and nothing eases the pain. Nothing lets me sleep.'

There were tears on Tinna's cheeks because she was remembering the way he had touched his hand to his daughter's gravestone. So very gently. She could smell salt and blood, and realised she was humming the lullaby again. Mazes and locked doors and longing.

'It never stops hurting,' she said.

'Never,' the man said. 'She was stolen from me. You understand. I only want what I am owed.'

Tinna nodded, she did. Death and memories; a twofold theft. The waves climbed the rock. 'What will it take to bring them back?' She hadn't intended to ask, only to follow. But the words were out before she could capture them.

'Blood and bone.'

She shook her head sadly, feeling older than the sea. 'It doesn't work,' she whispered. The aurora spiralled green, vermilion, lilac pathways across the vastnesses of space. 'I will bleed if I need to. But I *have* bled and been broken, and it doesn't work.'

'Not your blood, not your breaking. Where is the vengeance in that?'

She frowned, blinked. Not hers?

'Are you not hurting? Are you not angry?' The waves climbed her rock, furled around her ankles like claws, gripped tight.

She sighed, the sea sighed. 'Yes,' she whispered. 'Oh, yes I am.' The universe owed her its sorrow perhaps, but it deserved her anger more. 'But—'

'Here,' the man said; he bent to the water and lifted his cupped hands, pale and scarred, droplets falling like moons. 'Drink this. It will help you remember.'

'Oh,' she whispered.

Here it was. The key, the hope, the door.

A sip of wine to bind a promise, a sip of blood to bind a soul. What better key was there? What use reality when she had the sea at night and a story brought to life by a whole family's wounds.

Ben, she thought, her whole heart bleeding. Ben, I'm so close. I am finding my way through my broken pieces and home to you. 'Yes,' she said, and bent to the man's upheld palms, auroras on the water within them and his skin against hers cold as winter stones. She drank. The man watched, sad and hungry. The sound of a door slamming shut echoed across the water.

'It will help,' the man repeated. The ocean in the bowl of his palms glistened like falling tears.

Tinna drank once more, then once more. Gagged on salt water, swallowed salt water, straightened. The man smiled and his hands were empty, and the sea burned in her blood; it wove itself through her like chains.

'*Tinna!*' someone shouted.

Tinna turned on her rock. Her mouth, her heart, were full of grief and the tides. Her whole body swayed with waves, her eyes were full of the night sky, incandescent with the fury of a distant sun. She would give anything to the sea if it would stop the pain. Ben, she thought, bleeding.

'You understand,' the man whispered. 'I am owed blood.'

'Blood,' Tinna whispered.

Lilith called her name again, and at last fear stirred beneath her skin like a fish. A tiny silvery fish swimming against a rising tide and the binding she had drunk.

'Whose blood?' she said, but no-one answered and when she turned the man had taken two steps back, the sea around his thighs, waiting. 'Whose blood?' she repeated. 'If I cannot give mine?' But her body was all darkness and echoes. The answer was there and not there, quicksilver, the salt on her tongue tying her to the sea, to the key she had been searching for all this time. 'How do I remember?' she said.

'Vengeance,' the sea murmured. 'Blood.'

Yes, of course, Tinna thought. Then, no. Vengeance? This was madness. This was drugs and injury and a story to console the bereaved; Lilith shouting her name now, half-sobbing, coming this way. Tinna turned towards her, getting her feet beneath her on the rock and standing, feeling the lure of the water like a tether on her bones.

'I don't want vengeance,' she whispered. 'I want to remember.'

And there, behind Lilith, playing out against the night sky, was Ben.

A shadow form, an echo. A moment of his laughing in a restaurant she did not remember.

'Ben,' she whispered.

'Tinna!' Lilith was closer now, just metres away across the snowy field, but Tinna was not looking at her aunt because that fragment, it was so close, he was *so close*.

The sea murmured and all the blood in Tinna's veins rose in synchrony with the waves, phantom memories hovered on the edges of her vision, flickering like starlight. The aurora curled around the dome of the sky like a great, bright hand and Tinna reached out to touch the shadow of the man she loved with all her heart.

'Tinna, come away. For god's sake, come away.' She was at the top of the bank, further along, searching as if Tinna on her rock were invisible in the darkness.

I am owed my payment, the sea whispered. *I promise.*

'I want to remember,' Tinna repeated, her voice cracking, turning from her aunt to the sea and the figure in the waves, waiting but not patiently.

Make payment. Then we will both have back what was taken.

Yes, she thought. The silver fear-fish quivered, flexed against the tide. Wait, Tinna thought. Wait. Another memory flickered, his voice in the hall at the end of a day. *Hey love, I come bearing teabags.* Her laughter. A tiny, flicker-faint, heartbeat touch of his hand against her right one, their fingers tangling.

The memories wavered, and she cried out. Somewhere the cat hissed and the aurora sang, and Tinna heard herself humming. Ben's voice joined in, low and soft and he would have been so beautiful, she thought, singing their children to sleep.

The wind tugged at her hand like a child. *Please*, it murmured, *let us sleep.*

Are you coming?

Yes, Tinna thought. Wait for me. I'm coming. And then she was stepping off the rock into the sea.

'Tinna, where are you? I can't see—'

'Here,' Tinna said. She did not know when she had started weeping. 'Isn't it beautiful tonight?'

'Please,' Lilith said. 'Come out. You aren't safe.' She had found Tinna finally, standing where the risen sea met the grass, her silhouette against the house light like a mockery of those shadow memories that were fading already, and Tinna would do anything. She would give anything. The drugs and the pain were making a labyrinth of her thoughts but she had asked the universe to show her, and it had answered.

Weeping, holding out a hand. Fear circling within her, because something was wrong. The aurora shone blood red, fire red, and the waves were all teeth and silver, but there was salt in her blood and she was nothing but a scarred thing in a scarred land, holding out a hand. 'I'm here, Lilith. Come help me.'

Lilith stepped forward, the sea around her ankles and Tinna could see her shaking. They were both shaking and Tinna wanted to stop, but couldn't. She would give anything, but she hadn't meant this…

'Leave her alone,' Lilith called in Icelandic. 'For god's sake haven't you taken enough? Leave us alone.'

I cannot sleep, the sea whispered.

'We cannot sleep,' Tinna echoed. 'We only want—' She stopped.

She didn't want *this*…

'Please Tinna. Come out.'

But was this even real? Or was this all some strange phantasmagoria born of trauma and the dark? Did it matter—if it was real would that change anything at all? The waves curled around her knees, her thighs, pain all along her right side and she could not stop weeping. Her tears the only warmth in the whole endless night.

'Come to me, Lilith. Help me remember. It's not dangerous, I only want to remember.'

I promise. The skin of the sea was all black and silver and silk, holding Tinna up gently, absorbing her tears like it did the whole world's.

Lilith stepped further into the water, shaking. Her hand outstretched. 'No, Tinna,' she whispered. 'Don't do this. Don't let him do this.'

The aurora cut waveforms in blood and water across the sky, his face was there in the shadows, his laughter *just there* waiting beneath the murmur of the sea that was a promise and a half-open door.

'If I can just remember, then it'll be okay,' Tinna whispered. 'The last thing he said to me, the last time I touched him, whether he died gently.' Lilith took another step forward, the waves murmured. 'Is that too much to ask? I love him so much, Lilith. I love him and I don't know if he knew that when he died.'

'Oh Tinna,' Lilith whispered. 'He knew. Of course he knew.'

'Help me remember,' Tinna said, and took her aunt's hand in her numb right one. The sea whispered and she could almost feel Lilith's hand in hers. It felt like her mother's. Like the ghost of her mother. We are all ghosts, Tinna thought, and we are all lost, and all of us in the end are taken by the sea. So what does it matter?

'Come, Lilith,' she whispered, tugging like the sea was tugging, Lilith stumbling and the waves tightening their grip. 'Come make payment, then we shall sleep.'

'Please,' Lilith said in Icelandic. 'Let us go.'

But Tinna did not want to let go of anything.

'*Vini mínum vagga ég í ró*,' she sang. Lilith tried to pull away. Tinna tightened her hold. '*En úti biður andlit á glugga*.'

The sea rose and the sea fell, the sky was an open wound. Tinna sang lullabies to a night that was full of weeping. And…

And a truck roared to a stop, a voice called a name full of fire and fury, full of love. Love and fire, Tinna thought, and the night sky wove waveforms across the stars and Tinna's song faltered. Ben's hand touched her cheek.

'Tinna,' he said.

The voice called again closer, and Lilith answered, 'Gerdie!', twisting in the water.

'Where are you?' another voice called, one that made no sense but cut through the truck lights and the darkness like a beacon. Tinna was not looking for any light except his though. Lilith gasped and tried to pull herself free, Tinna staggered but held on, the waves climbing their limbs enfolding them.

'Tinna, please,' Lilith said. 'What are you doing? There are no answers here—'

'I'm making payment. Then I can remember.' But it sounded strange on her lips, salt and blood tainted, and she could see the echo of his face against the great black cliffs, gentle and waiting, the ghost of a smile.

'The sea won't give you your memories. It will only take. It will take—'

'The sea understands.'

'So do I,' Lilith said. And she said it so certainly, so sadly that Tinna blinked, turned from the cliffs to study her aunt's face in the dark, the aurora reflected in her wide eyes like flames.

'Lilith! Tinna!'

'Gerdie,' Lilith whispered, and Tinna's bones shuddered at that word because there was no salt in it, or blood or darkness, there was only love.

'I'm so angry,' she whispered.

Lilith found her other hand, her left one and the contact was another knife wound because it was so much easier to buffer yourself against pain than it was kindness.

'I know,' Lilith said. She squeezed Tinna's left hand, and perhaps her right one, and then let her go and when had it become her holding Tinna and not the other way around? But now she took one step back through the restless sea. Those two voices called again from the field and a cat yowled long and furious. Tinna shook her head wordlessly. Lilith's eyes caught the stars and she took another step away. 'I'm going to Gerdie now; she fears for me. Look who has come for you. Come home, Tinna.'

But Tinna did not move and Lilith waited two more heartbeats then left her in the sea. The waves hissed and wept against the rocks and Ben's voice hummed wordlessly. Tinna watched the headlights that sliced a pathway across the grass, through it two people moving. Then Lilith running towards them and into one of the figure's arms. They held one another like a lock and a key, and the other carried on moving down to the sea and *Oh*, Tinna thought. *Oh*. Ben hummed softly with his breath in her hair.

We only want what is ours, the sea whispered.

Yes, Tinna thought. The tide tugged on her within and without, promises swimming beneath the sea's skin like sharks. I want what is mine, she thought.

But perhaps the sea always painted its answers darkly, swallowed up the falling snow and reflected nothing but the depths and the dying. And was that it? If she really was nothing but tears and bone then what would become of the rest? Where would her love sit in between the falling stars and the abyss? Where her hope?

We would give anything.

Yes. But not everything.

Silver fear and bitter salt swam through her veins, painting all her bones cold. The sea hissed and whispered, and her pulse beat in time with the waves.

'Tinna,' someone said from the water's edge. 'Oh Tinna.' And the water crackled like ice as this person pushed fast towards her.

Tinna turned her head a little and still couldn't believe it. *Look who has come for you,* Lilith had said, but it couldn't be true. This here so much harder to understand than the man had been, standing in the sea and asking for blood.

But she stared at the newcomer, and it stayed true.

'Hello Mum,' she said quietly.

'Why couldn't you—' her mother began, but everything about her was unfathomable—her face raw with urgency, her voice breaking, her here at all in the black sea of an abandoned home. 'Tinna, love, come away now. Nothing good can come from this.'

Up in the field Gerdie and Lilith came apart, then curved together, and perhaps we are always as precious as the last time we were held like that, Tinna thought. So…

'Mum,' she whispered, 'I just want some of him back. Is that so much to ask?'

But she had called her aunt into the water. What wouldn't she give?

Waves broke far offshore with a sound like thunder and defeat.

'He loved you so much,' her mother said. She reached out as if for Tinna's hand then let her arm fall again. 'That has to be enough.'

'But he left me,' Tinna whispered.

Her mother shook her head once, stars fell from her eyes and Tinna could not remember ever seeing her cry. 'That doesn't change how much he loved you.'

'Doesn't it?'

Tinna looked at Gerdie and Lilith, then over her shoulder to the empty sea and then back to her mother.

'Oh Tinna,' her mother said very slowly in a voice Tinna did not recognise at all. 'Leaving you would have been the hardest thing he ever did. Loving you was the easiest. I promise.'

I promise, whispered the waves. Ben's face flickered in her mind, his smile shining in the dark. Her mother watched her steadily, weeping, and lifted her hand again and this time did not drop it.

...So all that matters is that we were held once even if it was a long time ago? Tinna turned away to face the starlit ocean, cradled the sea within her fingers, felt the pain and the numbness and every shade in between.

We cannot sleep, the sea mourned softly.

No, Tinna thought, we cannot. At least not without dreaming. But she could dream, and she could dream his name, and she would bleed because that meant the wound was clean.

The sea wept because she was weeping, salt to salt and lost things to lost things, but she realised that the tide was falling away again slowly, called home by the moon. Not so lost, she thought, after all. And made of more than angry tears, more than broken bones.

And there he was again, his face in the dark car turned towards her. Shattered windows and rain falling and 'Tinna,' he said. She reached out her right hand, trailing saltwater and touched his cheek, and he sighed, and she watched him close his eyes as gently as if falling asleep, broken glass and black blood setting him amongst stars.

'Ben,' she said. 'Don't leave me.'

'Hush,' he said. He said, 'I'm right here.'

'Don't leave me.'

'Oh, elskan mín,' her mother whispered. 'I'm so sorry. Please come home.'

Tinna curled her numb fingers around a memory like glass and pressed her fist against her heart. 'I'm coming,' she replied.

The sea wept, the sea released her gently back to the fierce earth. She closed her eyes beneath a blazing sky, the whole of her broken heart salt-laden and remembering. And she reached out for the hand that was waiting.

Acknowledgements

With thanks to Dave Goodman, Nick Binge and T. H. Dray for critiquing a draft of this, and to Robbie Guillory & Francesca Barbini for all their support.

To Jared and Meghan for being there, and to Iceland, for lending me its beauty for a while.

Discover Luna Novella in our store:

https://www.lunapresspublishing.com/shop

Milton Keynes UK
Ingram Content Group UK Ltd.
UKHW040615240124
436603UK00004B/131

9 781915 556264